"Hold up, magician. By author[...] are commanded to stop!"

"See you in hell!" Magus yelled back. And up the cathedral steps he went, three at a time. The authorities poured up the steps after him, throwing pikes as they went. Magus ran harder. His chest began to ache.

Curses, yells, pike-clangs created an uproar behind Magus as he ran through the cathedral. He tasted the bile of panic in his mouth. A dagger had bitten a hunk out of his left cheek during the last skirmish just moments before. The pain blazed through him like a sudden fever. He toppled back against his pursuers.

Magus kicked, punched, writhed. Useless. The authorities used the butts of their pikes to bludgeon him down.

He tried to crawl up on his hands and knees. Magus thought briefly of Maya and Robin. Got away, did they? That was some good—

The authorities bludgeoned him again.

And once again.

Several more times.

His head burst with intense light and he slid to the floor, senseless.

Ace Books has published another novel by John Jakes:

WEAR A FAST GUN

THE PLANET WIZARD

JOHN JAKES

ace books

A Division of Charter Communications Inc.
A GROSSET & DUNLAP COMPANY
1120 Avenue of the Americas
New York, New York 10036

THE PLANET WIZARD

Copyright © 1969 by John Jakes

An ACE Book

Cover art by Alex Ebel

Appreciatively dedicated to
DON WOLLHEIM,
benefactor of science-fiction,
not to mention
one of its writers.

Reprinted in 1977
Printed in U.S.A.

PROLOGUE

IN THE BEGINNING was the Out-riding.

Age upon age ago, beyond even dim folk-memory, the new lightships carried man out past the point of all return to the slow-wheeling billions of stars of II Galaxy. Here, separated forever from the First Home, man again built worlds from raw planets.

Among the multitudes of planets and men there arose power. It lodged in the great houses, the great commercial corporations whose births on the First Home none could remember. The great houses expanded and extended their dominion, drawing planet to planet, culture to culture, man to man in a glittering technologic webwork flung from one dim end of II Galaxy to the other.

But the human kind is quarrel-prone, and quick to snatch power and suck out its bitter sweetness.

Planetary wars split and burned and wracked II Galaxy end to end.

The great houses fell, abandoned, and their ringing names became wild chords lost in the minds of a few roving madmen—the houses of Genmor and Threem,

Xero and Unilev, Stanol and Stanbrans and Arsgrat and Easkod.

For as man will do, man cursed the very houses which brought him riches. He cursed the plenty-makers as warmakers—since they were in truth both—and cast their people out, and abominated their names.

And then, in the two generations after the holocausts, the star worlds of II Galaxy began to fear what they could no longer understand or remember.

Now the great houses are in ruins. The descendants of the Prime Managers who guided them are outcasts. The separate star worlds are sunk into the bestial dark of fear and isolation. Mystics are everywhere, and superstition.

Nowhere does the wind of demon-fear and demon-hate blow colder than on Pastora, smaller of the two inhabited planets of the Graphos system at II Galaxy's far rim.

Originally planned as a kind of living museum, Pastora was built upon the model of a charming rural land pictured and described in a few moldering histories of the First Home. Now its tiny farms and cathedral towns swim in a fearful twilight. Its people live with numberless fears.

Greatest of the fears is the fear of the demons which inhabit the sister planet, Lightmark.

Passage to Lightmark is forbidden by Pastora's High Governors. But these simple, frightened men in monks' robes have come to realize that Pastora's resources are running out. They recall tales which said that, before the holocausts, Lightmark was the home of one of the greatest of all the commercial corporations.

And so the simple, trembling men in monks' robes wonder whether the demons of Lightmark could be exorcised, so that the planet could be reached, and explored, and—who can say?—perhaps even plundered.

Like the first reverberation of a great bell which will one day ring power from star to star, new history is about to begin. The ancestor of the first ruler of the loose confederation of star kings which will one day rule II Galaxy is waiting in rags to seize his birthright.

To bring the day of the Lords of the Exchange.

His face? His name? His history?

Wait.

First the demons of Lightmark must be exorcised.

While the High Governors of Pastora do not as yet know it, those they want for the task are three.

A girl called Maya.

A young fighting man of the house and lineage of Dragonard.

And, most of all, a wandering charlatan named Magus Blacklaw.

This is their adventure, at the beginning of the first age of the star kings of II Galaxy.

I

THEY HAD BEEN running, it seemed, well nigh forever. At least it felt that way to Magus.

His legs hurt. His lungs and throat burned, as though filled with an uncoughable smoke. Yellow road-dust kicked up by his jackboots powdered in his long, gray-flashed black hair. It nested in his bushy brows and spade beard. It even crept into the corners of his oddly angled, oddly commanding eyes with their hazel pupils flecked with purple.

"Eyes to make devils curl their tails," a drunken peasant had put it once. That was just before Magus cheerfully relieved him of nearly a hundred credits by promising not to stopper the poor wretch's soul inside a little pewter bottle.

Now the eyes of Magus Blacklaw searched the horizons, no longer bold, no longer merry.

No sign of pursuit to be seen. But plenty to be heard. The *cloppa-drum* of the huntsmen's mounts sounded steadily from behind. The huntsmen themselves were obscured by the gently rolling hills of the twilight countryside. Clear and sharp over the drumming came the snap of the needle-toothed jaws of their meccanodogs.

No wonder the huntsmen could adopt a leisurely pace. The sensors of the blue-metal dog-shaped machines were unerringly set to pick up the scent of quarry. The meccanodogs could be programmed for a variety of speeds. Magus judged that they were set near the lowest. The huntsmen were playing with him and his daughter, certain of a kill.

"Maya?" The usual resonance of his voice was gone, turned a little hoarse. "We'll stop at that foot-bridge ahead."

"Not for my sake," the girl answered. "They're closer now. Can't you hear them?"

Magus grumbled that he could. "The clear call of the ennobled race of man. Hunting his fellow man like a savage. Rot 'em all, the hypocritical bastards."

Magus and his daughter hurried on. The dusty yellow road ran along beneath fever trees. Beyond the trees, the horizons were blurring into purple mist. Graphos had sunk an hour ago. The first moon was up, a silver pellet in the north.

To the southeast, the general direction they'd been traveling since they began their flight at noon, a single hovel stood stark against the top of a hill. A bit of smoke curled from the chimney pot. Magus eyed it with a combination of longing and fury.

No use seeking sanctuary there. After dark, no householder's door on Pastora would be opened to a magician.

Suddenly Maya stumbled. Magus growled a surprised oath, spun to catch her. He was a shade too late. The girl sprawled in the yellow dust.

Quickly Magus knelt. He brushed the dust from her cheeks and the crown of her russet hair. She was quite a pretty girl, full-figured, with eyes that echoed the purple of his own. Her face was her mother's though, a woman dead since childbirth twenty years ago.

Magus had hardened his heart to that and many other memories. But somehow he couldn't harden it enough now.

The sight of his daughter all a-sprawl in the dust, her fine shepherdess skirt and blouse smeared and ripped, brought new anger.

Directed exclusively at himself.

"Here take my hand, Maya. We stop at the footbridge, dogs or no."

"Father, I swear I'm perfectly"—she breathed hard—"perfectly all right."

Her cheeks were warm. The color had left her lips. Her hair was a frightful tangle. He thought he saw a tear shining in one corner of an eye, moistening the yellow dust caught there.

"Your looks hardly support that statement."

He helped her up. She started to protest. He silenced her with another grumbled curse. All at once she admitted her weariness to herself and to him by slumping against him with a little forlorn cry.

Magus slipped his arm around her waist. Together they staggered toward the little footbridge that arched across the bubbling, nameless creek. Wildflowers shone like red and yellow gems in the lengthening shadows.

Dolt! Magus said to himself. *Numbskull! You've known for years that the yokels of New Delft are the most fanatical law-abiders among all the citizens of the market towns. After nearly forty years tramping this planet, you've yet to practice simple caution!*

Keep quiet! another part of him responded. *The burghers of New Delft are also among the richest on all Pastora. Highly susceptible to being fooled by a peerless prestidigitator who knows nothing at all about true magic—the powers which make things like those damn meccanodogs run—but everything about speaking to the fears of the gullible in order to part him from credits—*

Spare me your rhetorical gas, his angry self replied. *You're a worthless fool.*

The hell you say. I'm Magus Blacklaw! Wencher extraordinary. Trencherman of note. Damn accomplished swordsman—

A thin, keen blade bobbed at his hip as he guided Maya the last few staggering steps to the footbridge. The night air was beginning to bite with chilliness. Behind, the hoofpads of the beasts went *cloppa-drum.* The jaws of the meccanodogs clacked like the blades of freshly sharpened scissors. The pursuers were still out of sight.

Despite all you say, the furious side of himself took up, *you lack brains. To avoid New Delft would have been prudent—*

Stop preaching, you pious bag of starch! The experience had its virtues—

He left Maya sitting spent on the stone rail of the bridge and scrambled down the bank to fetch up some water in a little leathern cup he carried at his studded belt. With considerable warmth he recalled the widow Serafina.

Warm, comely, buxom and about his own age, she had gorgeous hair of the same red-sable color as Maya's mother. She gave Magus the lizard-neck pack beast that carried them for the first three hours of their flight. Not accustomed to bearing two riders for long, the beast threw them at the end of that time and hammered away over the hills.

The widow Serafina's generosity made it possible for them to get a good start on their pursuers. The bailiff's huntsmen took their own cruel time in gathering and switching on their meccanodogs.

Some of the water in the cup spilled over his dusty hands as he reached the bridge. The water felt piercingly cool. Knowing that the meccanodogs would run them down and bite them to death with their needle teeth was the same kind of sensation.

Magus scratched his left eye, scanned the darkening horizon as Maya drank. Her shoulders slumped. All at once she seized his black-haired hand. She bent, sobbing.

"Father—I can't help it—I'm so tired—"

Desperation beat inside his head like a caged bird.

"We won't die," he said. Then, louder, "We won't die tonight, I promise you."

Saying it was far easier than making it a fact.

Think, man! You're her father. It's you who led her into this rotten life of following a false wizard from tavern to scummy tavern—

Be quiet!

I will not! If you weren't such a damned lecher and hadn't spent last night in frivolous frolic with that widow, your wits would have been sharper in the market square this morning. You'd have spied that bailiff clinging to the inn gable behind you. A skillful wizard never, never allows a bailiff to observe him from behind—

5

Along the northern horizon the pack of meccanodogs appeared on the yellow road. Their electrified eyes shone like small, fiercely cold amber stars.

The mechanical beasts ran with an odd jerking motion. Their metal flanks and squarish heads caught the first beams from the second moon's rising. The bailiff and his huntsmen cleared the crest of the distant hill and reined in their lumbering beasts. The meccanodogs loped steadily ahead.

"So that's the game," Magus said. "They stay safe and watch their tin killers finish us. Quick, Maya. Stand up, *Stand up!*" He seized her arm too hard. She cried out.

It was nearly dark. The peasant's hovel on the other horizon could barely be seen. Magus quickly apologized to Maya, leading her on across the footbridge. The scissors-clack of the jaws of the meccanodogs grew louder. Another half or three-quarters of a league at most and the dozen snapping, murdering contraptions would be on them.

Maya's voice rose hysterically, not making sense. She stopped, struggling, in the center of the bridge.

"Don't do that, girl! We must keep going!"

But it was a futile exercise in self-preservation at best.

As he struggled with her, the leathern strap of his light pack slipped from his left shoulder. The pack dropped over the bridge rail into the water, making a loud splash.

"Stand here, Maya! *Stand!*"

The girl stared at him, still sobbing.

"My pack's in the water. The water'll ruin everything in it—"

And over the edge of the bridge Magus went, landing with a jar on the slippery stones.

He'd gone after the pack without so much as thinking about it. That pack was his most precious possession, his only means of livelihood. It contained his single good robe of black iricloth that shimmered with a weird chameleon display of colors in the proper light; his red sash silverstitched with cabalistic symbols; his bunches of colored silks; his packets of green powder for materializing fireballs; and several other simple but useful pieces of gimmickry.

The big, stoutly-built man plunged his hands into the cold water, caught the pack and hefted it. At the same instant he realized the meaning of what he'd shouted to Maya.

The water will ruin everything.

Magus bolted up the creek bank and around onto the bridge. He caught Maya's wrist. He pulled her after him, down off the bridge to the thick sward where the wildflowers grew.

The meccanodogs were drawing close, flashing down the center of the road. Their amber eyes blazed. Magus could even see the little silver filamants, their sensing antennae, springing from their metal muzzles.

Running like a wild man with Maya stumbling along behind, Magus tried to remember. He was certain as he could be. In a drunken effort to explain the inner working of the meccanodogs, a friendly bailiff had once told him that their one point of fallibility in a cross-country chase was their susceptibility to damage by—

"Father, where are we going?" Maya cried, tugging against him.

"Stop your caterwauling!"

His voice was loud. It hit her like a blow. Her eyes flew all the way open. All at once she stopped crying.

He released her, feeling very proud of her suddenly. She was very tough. She'd come through all that had happened today, all the leagues of running, with only this single sobbing breakdown when tiredness got the worst of her. He snatched her up in both his arms and went splashing across the creek.

"We're going where"—he gasped out the words—"any good but dusty girl goes, pet. To . . . take a little . . . bath."

They reached the opposite bank of the creek. Magus carried her to the top of a low hill. He let her down and turned back toward the yellow road, the bridge and the bank of the creek they had just crossed.

Far away, the huntsmen seemed to be stirring on their mounts. Did they sense something awry? The meccanodogs reached the bridge. They bunched together in a nervous, circling pack at the far edge. The silver antennae on their muzzles flickered in the crisscrossing rays of the two moons, which had now been joined by a third, three pearls riding upward in different quarters of a deep blue silk sky.

On the bank, the amber eyes of the meccanodogs shone.

Magus felt an awful sweat on his palms. If this failed, they would die with those needle teeth digging into their throats. There was little strength left in him, and none at all in Maya, who lay at his feet.

"Smell us," Magus whispered at the metal dogs snapping down there. It was the only form of praying he knew. "Smell us, you filthy tinheads, *smell us!*"

A metal muzzle lifted and flashed cold in the light of

the three moons. The filament antennae quivered. Other heads in the pack came up.

The first meccanodog ran jerkily down the bank, stopped, raised its head again. The amber eyes shone like smudged lanterns, brilliant in the nearly total darkness.

The meccanodog opened its jaws and shut them. This close, it sounded like a blade slicing clean through bone. The dog leaped.

It hit the water at exactly the spot where Magus had crossed. The other meccanodogs followed. They jammed together in a pack. Just as the last one stepped into the water, the first one reached the creek's midpoint. Trailing sour-smelling smoke, it exploded.

With a series of flat, spitting reports, the meccanodogs blew apart. Hunks of metal and flurries of pink sparks showered all over the creek banks. Magus took a sharp blow from a piece of flying debris with twenty-four burned-out colored wires hanging from it. In another moment the dogs were all gone.

On the near bank a single complete metal head lay twisted off its body. It emitted a buzzing and grinding. The jaws worked once, twice. The amber eyes dimmed out. The metal skull shone dead under the three moons.

Magus reached out to stroke his daughter's cheek. "Up, girl. A little further is all now. Till we find a safe nook. The huntsmen won't come after us in the dark without their killers."

Gradually Maya realized they had won a reprieve. She hugged against him, actually managing a little laugh. Magus helped her walk as they hurried on across the next hill.

"You're a clever man, Father."

"No, but I've a good head for odd facts. I have no idea what makes a meccanodog work. Some of the magic from before the nuclear rains, no doubt. But I did remember being told that their innards couldn't stand water without fatal damage. That's all."

False modesty. Magus really felt rather proud of himself.

In a short time they reached a small copse. Magus took off his outer tunic of leather and wrapped it around his shivering daughter. He listened. No *cloppa-drum* at all.

He sank down to rest. A sudden moodiness came over him.

And then depression. It was unlikely that the bailiff of New Delft would give up the pursuit altogether. Magus and Maya stood a fine chance of being hounded for days, weeks, months. It wearied him to think about it.

He glanced down. Maya had fallen asleep against his chest. She looked quite lovely in the moonlight drifting between the slender trunks of the trees. Dirty-cheeked and tattered, yes. But lovely. A woman. With her life ahead of her.

What sort of life? Magus asked himself. His mouth twisted in self-contempt as he leaned back and breathed the night air.

What sort of life could there be ahead of her with the bailiff's huntsmen still behind?

More running? More taverns? More sleazy crowds? Till when, Magus Blacklaw?

Till you're dead and she's as old and lonely as you?

The reprieve forgotten, Magus Blacklaw looked squarely at a future that looked bleak indeed.

II

IN THE NEXT few hours, as Maya slept snuggled against his shoulder, Magus confronted himself and his situation with an unusual honesty.

It wasn't pleasant. But something inside him demanded he do it. Perhaps the near-kill by the meccanodogs had pulled him back to reality in a way nothing else could have done.

He didn't like facing the truth about himself. But it was better to do it now, in a moment of peace in the moonpearled copse, than drag Maya through another spate of years of aimless living.

The bearded man stared pensively at the hard stars beyond the shivering treetops. A breeze had risen again, quite cool. It blew from the south. It carried a strange sound which Magus finally recognized as the bleating of sport sheep.

So there was a flock yonder across the dark hills? That meant a shepherd too. Then it would be best to swing wide when they resumed their journey in the morning. The shepherd lads who tended the huge flocks of mutant sheep were seldom bright. But they knew enough to raise halloos when suspicious strangers passed.

No telling when that stranger might be a sorcerer, eh?

In the moon-dapple, Magus' mouth twisted again.

His father had died in his middle manhood, a land-tiller all his life. But the elder Blacklaw had owned a few precious possessions—book-rolls saved by Magus' grandparents when they fled the nuclear rains during the wars that had ended about fifty-five years ago.

Magus had been taught to read by his mother. She lived four years after his father died of accelerated senility at age forty-two. That was another effect of the rains.

The book-rolls were mostly fictions, plus a couple of geographies of Pastora which had evidently once been school texts. Long ago someone had ripped out all the pages of the geographies which dealt with the system's companion planet, Lightmark. Even today Magus couldn't keep back a shudder when he thought of that hidden-away world which no one visited.

Sometimes, at the right star-seasons, Lightmark was visible to the naked eye. It shone faintly purple-red in the north-eastern quadrant of the heavens. In his travels Magus had heard a few hard-eyed adventurers claim that wealth lay waiting for anyone who would venture to Lightmark to claim it. This wealth supposedly took the form of various assets of a great commercial house destroyed or at least depopulated in the nuclear rains.

Since the adventurers invariably told their stories while attired in filthy rags, Magus disbelieved.

Everyone said Lightmark was accursed. Peopled with demons whose fantastic appearance was glibly described by peasants who had never seen them. Magus supposed the demons were imaginary. His education from book-rolls before his mother died, and an education of a more practical sort which he undertook when he ran away from his mother's gravestone to follow and apprentice with the old wizard Phlebos, had lent him a certain skepticism. He considered himself mentally a cut above most of the planet's peasants.

Still, it was never wise to condemn demons one had never seen.

He traveled with old Phlebos until the latter died. By then Magus was in his early twenties. He'd learned enough of the old man's tricks so that he could take them over for himself.

Old Phlebos of the purple-gray beard had been an entertainer. He'd been content to perform in the market and cathedral towns and eke his living from the few ha'credits tossed into the bandanna Magus carried into the audience at the end of every performance. Quicker of mind, Magus saw a better way to utilize the tricks that became his when Phlebos died.

Magus didn't abandon crowds entirely. But he preferred playing to an audience of one, manipulating fireballs created from the greenish powder he compounded afresh every month or so. Alone with his victim, Magus would convince the rich countryman that he could transport the countryman's immortal soul to Lightmark, imprisoned in a fireball, where it would dwell forever. Unless, of course, the countryman rewarded him generously.

He'd never been disturbed overmuch by his own lack of scruples. Let those who would not be fooled educate themselves out of foolishness. But he was growing tired of the endless traveling. And the fakery had consequences, as he had discovered again today, that could be drastic.

"You're losing your sense of humor," he muttered to himself. Maya stirred against his shoulder.

He tried to think of pleasant things.

Wenches.

The widow Serafina.

How good ale tasted.

The smell of charcoal chips smoldering on the hearth of an inn in the deep of a winter's night.

The satisfaction of using his thin, keen sword expertly against some country braggart twice his weight and half his wits.

All these were satisfying to him once. They might be so again. But not now, not now.

The wind was rising. It carried the bleats of the sport sheep hidden by the hills southward. It carried the chill of age.

Magus Blacklaw past his prime? Gods, no, not yet. Not for a long time yet. But he was older. And he did have responsibilities to Maya. All at once, he found himself wishing that he could suddenly amass a great tally of credits. He'd buy a country estate, retire and raise sport sheep himself.

For a moment his teeth blazed in a white grin through his beard. Then the smile vanished.

Who are you gulling, lout? There's no way you can amass credits, and there's no other life for which you're suited or trained.

Frustrated and then angered, Magus thought of scheme after scheme. None made sense. Especially not with the uncertainty of the immediate future.

The bailiff and his men from New Delft might continue the pursuit or they might not, depending upon their whim. Magus found himself a man neatly boxed by his past, his age, his limited skills.

And yet, for the first time in years, he was seized by a desperate compulsion to do something for Maya. Make her life better. Break this pattern of sleeping in the open and living by wits alone.

No way of escape from the situation suggested itself. This soon brought him back to a state of dismal brooding. Perhaps in the morning he'd think of something. There had to be something . . .

Down went his head. Merciful sleep wiped out a mangled yesterday and an uncertain tomorrow alike.

Just before dawn Magus bolted up, eyes wide. His hand clawed for the basket-hilt of his sword.

Then he realized that it was his daughter who had made the noise. While he slept she had risen, moved away from him. Now she stood limned against tree-trunks and lightening sky, rubbing her forearms to restore some warmth.

She smiled. It was good to see.

"I didn't mean to wake you, Father."

Magus clicked his sword back into its sheath. "In another moment I'd have spitted you through the stomach and damned you for a bailiff." He walked over and put his arm around her. "How do you feel?"

"Much better."

"We'd best make plans. Not only for a fast departure here but for—after."

"Will the huntsmen follow us?"

"I'd judge the chances are split about even."

"I—wanted to tell you how sorry I was for acting as I did last night. Crying and—"

"Hush, Maya. It's a woman's place to sob when

circumstances bedevil her. It's a man's place to find the ways to save her from the crying. You'll learn that when you have your own husb—''

He chopped off the word, wishing he hadn't said it. Maya would have no chance whatever of finding a suitable young man if she were forever tramping after a father whose sole destiny seemed equally divided between poverty, arrest and liquidation.

Maya sensed Magus' discontent with himself. "Where are we going now?" she asked.

"Well, that's a bit of a problem. Normally I'd say we should keep straight on along the yellow road. A few more leagues would put us in New Brussels."

"A large town. Such a pretty cathedral."

"And plenty of pretty peasant purses to help fatten ours. Again I'm just not sure whether it's wise to go there."

Thinking, Maya finally said, "There are no other large cities with a hundred leagues. New Brussels looks to be our best chance. And just about our only one."

Magus was forced to nod. "We can't survive in open country forever. Yet there would be risks in New Brussels too. The huntsmen will ride directly there if they come after us. On the other hand, there's a certain safety in crowds—"

His words drifted off again. He didn't like the idea of heading for the large cathedral town. But the more he thought it over, the more it seemed the only avenue left open to them. They were nearly down to their last ha'credit. Yes, New Brussels, despite its potential dangers, would have to be—

A shard of fire ripped the sky open, lighting Maya's upturned face pale red.

She pointed. "What is that thing, Father?"

Something streaked from the high heavens toward the earth. Magus had only an instant in which to judge its shape and size. Short. Black. Streamlined. All at once, it seemed to decelerate. Then it vanished behind a southern hill. An explosion blasted the dawn. A green-shot orange corona burst up behind the hillside. More grinding and crashing followed. The light-flares widened. The bleating of the sport sheep grew much louder.

"That was a skysled," Magus breathed. "One- or two-man."

"But it was out of control."

"Yes, and the pilot's probably dead from the crash. As fas as I could tell it was unmarked." Calculating swiftly, Magus added. Let's find it, Maya. We may be able to help the pilot. And depending on where it came from, we may be able to find things in the wreckage we can use. Supplies, food—"

Magus slung his pack over his shoulder and started from the copse with Maya hurrying at his side. The sky was very light on the horizon now, a brilliant water-color blue. Magus swung out in long steps through the heavy sward. Maya kept up.

"No markings?" she said all at once. "That means it was—"

"Stolen from the High Governors and all the marking painted out. An illegal flight by someone who knew how to operate its thinking-machine controls."

A little tic of dread bothered Magus' cheek as he said that. There were very few skysleds left on Pastora since the holocausts. Whoever had flown this one was a lawbreaker of the worst sort. Magus kept a sharp eye on the circle of the sky in case the thief had stolen his craft only a short time ago from one of Pastora's cities. That would bring a small flock of official pursuit vehicles chasing after.

Father and daughter raced up a long, gently sloping hillside. Maya screamed.

"Dammit, girl, don't yowl at the slightest—" Words froze like iceballs in his mouth.

Over the hill's summit thundered a gigantic woolly sport ram, its cornucopia horns giving off bluish light and its swollen, filmy eyes rolling.

The ten foot tall ram bleated deafeningly and charged straight at them.

The rest of the flock of sports, some twenty or thirty in all, trampled along right behind. They spilled down the hillside in a woolly wave. Magus slammed against Maya and flung her to the ground.

The ram blundered past. Magus bowed his head, covering it with his arms until most of the flock had gone by. He jumped up again. A giant ewe buffeted him, knocking him off balance.

All at once Magus heard a sharp cry. A man came bounding around the slope of the hill to Magus' left. The man ran straight toward the stampeding flock. He was young, barefoot, yellow-haired, clad in a waist-wrapping of animal skin. A black finger ring flickered dully in the dawn as he brandished a sword at the ram charging in the lead, pricking its snout.

"Turn back! Turn back!"

The young man shouted oaths of such color that Magus knew he was not merely a simple shepherd, but had at least some schooling in the more sophisticated, civilized ways. *Whick-whack* went the shpherd's blade as he ran in among the sports. He stung their snouts with the sword-tip to turn them aside.

18

The shepherd continued to hop up and down, gesture violently, curse at the top of his lungs and lay about with the sword until the leaders of the flock started to mill. Magus watched with some awe. The shepherd was brave, for he must have been near-blinded by the accumulated bluish light pouring off the horns of the giant rams.

Just at the moment when it seemed that the shepherd had quieted his runaway flock, his bare right foot disappeared into the earth.

"Stepped into a fur-burrow!" Magus exclaimed.

Down went the shepherd, cursing louder than ever. His flailing right hand lost control of the sword. It raked the flank of a ewe, biting deep. Phosphorescent bluish blood welled up through the tight wool. The ewe rolled her great half-blind eyes and began to turn in a tormented circle.

She crashed against the others of the flock. In an instant the rams were bellowing again.

Magus had only a fragmentary view of the shepherd. He'd thrown his sword aside and was fighting to wrench his foot from the fur-burrow.

"He'll be trampled!" Maya cried.

That takes no especial intuition to discover, Magus thought. But he forgave Maya her womanly outburst, even as he shucked off his sword belt, kicked off his jackboots and ran as fast as he could toward the wildly milling flock.

III

THE SHEPHERD LOOKED out between the thrashing legs of
the sheep and saw Magus coming. His strong-featured
face shone with hope, just as a terrified ram smashed
his horny hoof against the shepherd's temple.

The shepherd tumbled over backward. Magus
scrambled in beneath the dangling teats of a ewe, then
dropped to all fours. He crawled fast. He reached the
shepherd and tugged the caught foot free so violently
that the lad yelped.

"Tha—thank—" the shepherd began.

"Save your tongue and watch your head!"

Magus pushed the younger man sideways as a ram
stamped down, smashing the ground where the
shepherd's left leg had been a moment before.

Sheep at the edge of the milling flock began to amble
off. The shepherd started to crawl after them. Magus
held him back.

"Let them run away from us. Less chance of one of
our heads getting popped."

"But it's my only flock! If I lose them, I've nothing
left—"

A ewe kicked the shepherd nearly unconscious. He

pitched over on his side, wobbling his head and cursing in frustration. By the time he finally got to his feet the sport sheep were scattering outward in a ragged circle.

Moments later the last ram disappeared over a hill-crest. Its horns gave off only a faint bluish glow in the lightening sky.

Magus stood up. He dusted his tunic and smoothed his beard. Maya ran up carrying her father's jackboots and sword belt.

"Young man," said Magus, "you appear to have lost your livelihood. But you are still alive."

Down the morning wind drifted a raucous bleat. The shepherd cursed vividly.

"May I remind you," Magus said, "that you are in the presence of a young woman."

The shepherd flushed. He walked over to retrieve his sword.

"Apologies," he said.

"Accepted. I'm Magus Blacklaw. This is my daughter Maya." The wizard had already decided that he liked the cut of the shepherd's face. Besides the lad would hardly betray someone who had just saved his life.

The shepherd returned with his blade. Magus noted certain rusty-colored stains upon it. But on reflection that wasn't surprising. Despite his youth, the shepherd looked formidable.

Sun had burned him very dark, and bleached his hair yellow-white. Magus judged him to be a few years older than Maya. The younger man saluted them both with his sword. For the first time Magus got a clear look at the lad's strange golden eyes.

"I thank you both," the shepherd said. "The sled that came down frightened the flock."

"Ah yes, the sled," Magus said. "We were on our way to the wreckage when we saw you."

"On your way to the wreckage from where?"

"From where we came from."

Magus' words were faintly defiant, testing the lad. Abruptly his belly growled. He was sure Maya was equally hungry. They couldn't walk on to New Brussels unfed. Well, why not risk it?

"Lad, do you have anything to eat? I'm a traveling wizard, you see. My daughter and I have run short of supplies temporarily—"

The shepherd's golden eyes slitted down. "A wizard? I saw one once when my uncle took me to the marketplace in New Delft. My uncle said all wizards were fakers."

"Your uncle is no friend of mine." Having decided that he was dealing with a young man of reasonable intelligence and honesty, not a peasant clod, Magus found it easy to smile and add, "despite the fact that he was quite correct."

The shepherd regarded Magus a long moment. Then the stern wariness of his tanned face relaxed. He smiled too, wiping a smear of blood from his left temple. "To answer your question, I've got a little saltmeat and some wine at my camp. You're welcome to it."

"Excellent! First, though, let's see to the skysled."

Maya was watching the lad with a keen interest. "You haven't told us your name. Or whether you and your uncle live near here."

"To answer the last first," replied the shepherd, "my uncle has been gone from Pastora nearly six years.

He was a man of some learning, you see. He didn't like the way of life on Pastora since the wars. We come of an old family. He told me tales of how my grandfathers traded on the planets that are supposed to lie beyond our own sun. Well, my uncle stole a government skysled and rode it out there''—a slash of an arm toward the sky—''to try to reach another world.''

''Another world?'' Magus exclaimed. ''Lightmark?''

''They say Lightmark is cursed. He went beyond. To find worlds the yokels of Pastora deny exist any longer. I stayed behind because he said I was too young. I'm sure my uncle's never coming back. He's probably dead. I've been tending this flock—I built it up from strays—until the day when I was old enough to decide what my course should be. Whether to follow my uncle, or—'' The golden eyes clouded. ''Whatever. Now it appears the decision's been forced on me. So perhaps I'll join you and walk the road as far as New Brussels if you're heading there.''

Maya threw a quick, questioning look at her father. Magus decided swiftly.

''Yes. We are. There are certain—advantages—in the city for a person in my line of work.''

Such as crowds to hide you.

The morning countryside was still except for a long birdcall over the crackle of flame from the wrecked skysled. All this open space made him nervous. He hitched up his sword belt, glancing at the ring which the shepherd wore on the last finger of his right hand.

It was wrought of gold, with an oval black stone. The stone's long dimension paralleled the bone of his finger. Into the black stone were etched images of two mythical beasts, a snarling lion and a rising phoenix. Something about it made Magus' scalp crawl. He pointed.

"I've seen that mark, shepherd. In a book-roll long ago. Your people were freebooters . . .?"

"Some." The gold eyes turned wary again. The shepherd's hand tightened, whitened on the hilt of his sword. "It's said some were princes, and some profiteers. There are many tales—"

"That ring is the sign of your house, isn't it?"

"Yes," said the shepherd. "The house of Dragonard."

Maya's gasp was just audible.

To those blessed with the ability to read the old rolls, the name Dragonard had a mythic ring. The Draonards were folk-figures. One of the geographies Magus had read in his youth contained references to the family. At last he'd actually met one of them! Human enough, even though the shepherd was a little larger than life in his muscular tallness.

"Tell us your first name," Maya said.

A wash of red swept up the shepherd's throat to the point of his chin. "It's Robin."

The guffaw from Magus was quite involuntary. He'd hardly anticipated such a gentle first name for a lad so tough and brawny. He doubled over, trying to bring his laughter under control. Something cold-sharp whickered under his chin and touched there, hurting.

The point of Robin Dragonard's sword pricked the magician's wind-toughened neck.

"Stop your laughing or I'll kill you."

Very slowly Magus straightened up. He moved his hands outward from his body to signify peace. This was odd, puzzling and—the more he thought about it—infuriating.

Robin kept the sword-point tight against Magus' throat. The magician croaked out: "I apologize, lad! But your reaction is unwarranted."

His gold eyes steady and fierce, Robin replied, "There are very few things that will provoke my temper, Magus Blacklaw. But that's one of them. My name is my name. Admitted, it's a little too light for anybody who thinks of himself as a man. But it's the only name I have. If you want to make sport of it, be prepared to answer."

It was Maya who managed to break the tension. "Robin sounds fine and strong to me."

"Thank you," he said stiffly. "Unfortunately that opinion isn't widely held by the peasants in the neighborhood. They go by names like Thurd and Sworg." He relaxed a little, the fury draining out of him. He fixed Magus with his keen gold eye and gave the sword-point a little twist. "But what's your final opinion, wizard?"

Magus liked the shepherd more every moment. He was a fighter. Not afraid to defend his ideas, however unusual they might be. This was a sharp contrast to most of the inhabitants of Pastora. They were willing to be frightened into accepting almost any idiot dictum so long as they saved their own smelly hides in the process. Magus grinned and took one sudden step back away from the sword-point.

"A man's name isn't half as important as what kind of man he is, Robin Dragonard. You seem the right sort. Let's agree that my opinion of your name doesn't really matter."

That brought an agreeable expression to Robin's face. "Accepted, wizard. Now—"

"The skysled," Maya reminded them.

Magus nodded. "Yes, we've lost a great deal of time already. Let's see whether the pilot's still alive."

They plowed up the hillside and down its far slope. From there they headed at an oblique angle toward the top of a much larger eminence. Maya had to run to keep up with the two men. They swallowed up the wind-tossed grass in huge strides. As they went, Robin said: "The pilot will be better off dead if any but us find him. That sled was stolen."

"So you noticed the lack of markings too? Magus said.

Maya tugged at Magus' sleeve. "Father?"

He stopped, facing round to her impatiently.

"Girl, if some poor sod is bleeding his guts away waiting for help, we shouldn't waste—"

"This is important. We're going to New Brussels and this young man wants to go with us. Before he does, you should give him the chance to change his mind. Now, before he feels any more beholden to us. Tell him why we're hurrying to the town."

Nettled, Magus retorted, "You've become quite concerned for his welfare all of a sudden."

Maya's violet eyes caught the blazing sun. "I have a concern for telling the truth, Father."

Robin looked perplexed. "What's she talking about?"

Magus shrugged. "She wants me to tell you that you might not wish to associate with us after all. Nor even feed us at your campsite later. We're not exactly racing across the countryside by choice. In New Delft I had an

26

unfortunate—ah—encounter with the authorities. They sent huntsmen after us. Plus a pack of their metal dogs, which I dispatched last night. I don't think we're being pursued at the moment. But that doesn't mean we're safe. Maya wants you to understand the whole situation, I believe.''

Amused, Robin studied father and girl. ''Trouble with the authorities. Did they make the same discovery my uncle did? That wizards sometimes trick—?''

''Careful,'' Magus warned. ''I'm not sensitive about my name. But in certain areas I react most unpleasantly.''

Robin tossed his head back and laughed. ''I like you, Magus Blacklaw. You're a man of brains and a little bit of humor too. Thank you for telling me the truth. Let the clods be bilked! I've no respect for them. It's their own damned fear of learning that keeps them bound up in superstition and makes them easy prey for men like y—that—'' Robin coughed to cover the rest. Then he resumed: ''I haven't any quarrel with what you do, Magus. I quarrel with this whole benighted planet and the way it hides from the truth of things. Besides, I'm not frightened of the authorities. Of course I'll go on with you.''

''And welcome, then,'' Magus told him with real feeling.

As they moved toward the hilltop again, Robin walked beside the girl. ''I thank you too, Maya, for wanting the truth out.''

Gods almighty, the wench is blushing! Magus watched from a corner of an eye.

Maya said softly, ''It was the only right thing, Robin Dragonard.''

Rather than be reduced to cynical snickering by the clumsy little exchange, Magus found himself moved. And reminded again of the pressing necessity to provide something better for her than a life of endless running.

The shepherd? Naturally not. The lad was a brawler. Belonging to the Dragonards, he'd probably die young, gutted in a quarrel or worse. But it was gratifying to see that Maya could attract the notice of men her age. Magus hadn't roughened and toughened her past all femininity. At least not yet.

Robin ran ahead up the hillside. "I smell burning."

A poisonous little plume of saffron-colored smoke drifted from the other side. As Magus and his daughter reached the crest behind Robin, they saw the source of it.

The skysled, roughly ten times longer than a tall man was tall, had crumpled to the earth in the hollow at the hill's base. Mangled metal fins and struts thrust up every which way. The whole control canopy at the forward end had ruptured, spilling the innards of the thinking-instruments. Spiderwebs of orange and yellow and green and purple wire leaked the saffron smoke. Over the whole wreckage hung a stink of roasting and dying.

"Where's the man who flew the thing?" Maya asked as the trio started down.

Robin pointed suddenly. "Thrown clear. There on the other side. Behind that bent vane."

They circled warily around the destroyed skysled. Magus regarded the craft with a certain superstitious awe. A deep, agonized groan drifted on the morning breeze. Just at the moment he heard it, Magus spied the pilot lying on the sward a short distance from the wreck.

The man's one-piece light blue garment shone sticky with great wine-colored patches at chest, belly and groin. He was on his back. His mountainous bloodied belly puffed up and down, up and down with the force of his injured breathing. More blood dribbled in thin lines from under the right cuff of his garment.

The man was bald, middle-aged. A scar puckered his cheek. The blunt place at the point of his jaw bore another, older scar, neatly triangular. Magus recognized the mark.

"Branded freebooter," he whispered to Robin. "That little blue triangle on the chin means he was caught by the High Governors once. His skin was burned and injected with a dye so he'd be known wherever he went."

"Poor man," Maya said. "He's still alive."

They approached the bleeding hulk. Maya knelt beside him. She began to pick at the chest fastenings of his garment, trying to get at the wounds. Magus crouched across from her. He was very proud of his daughter at this moment. She showed no reaction to the blood except a slight paleness. *I've taught her a few things well.*

The death-swollen man let out a cry. His fat eyelids flew back. Maya drew her hand away.

"I didn't mean to hurt you."

"Authorities," the fat man said. A little blood-bubble formed at the corner of his hip. *"Authorities—!"*

Gently Magus pushed the straining bulk back down. "No. Just travelers. Pilgrims."

"Help me. Help me, won't you? I'll be all right with

some medication—'' The man's smeared red hand lifted in the direction of the wrecked sled. ''Name's Huygens. Hans Huygens. Too old to wrestle one of those alone. Lost control of 'er coming back into the atmosphere. The guidance went out. Managed to slow 'er down on manual at the last minute so I didn't get killed when she hit.''

He struggled up again. His small brown eyes were bright, full of hurt.

''Please. Medication. I'll be perfect with some medi—''

He fell back gasping. Across the mound of stomach Magus looked at Robin. In those gold eyes he saw the truth he already knew.

The freebooter Huygens was broken apart inside. Hadn't a chance.

Magus made his lie glib and believable:

''Of course you'll make it. We'll help you. But this is important. Will there be any sleds from the towns coming after you?''

''Don't . . . think so. Stole the sled . . . week and more ago. From the government pool at New Cologne. Wasn't . . . easy. Authorities . . . all over the place. But . . . I had to take the risk. Getting . . . to be an old man. Not . . . many chances left. And the stories nearly drove me crazy. Had . . . to find out whether there were . . . all those treasures . . . hidden up there the way the peasants say. . . .''

''Treasures?'' Magus blinked. ''Hidden up where?''

Huygens struggled to answer. All that came out was a wicked bubbling sound.

Robin laid his hand on the fat man's shoulder. This calmed Huygens a little. Robin bent forward until the fat man could stare up directly into the gold eyes. Robin asked:

"If you didn't come from a town with the stolen sled, where did you come from?"

The blue-dyed triangle on Huygen's chin popped with tiny diamonds of sweat. His hand flipflopped in the sward, then lifted at the sky and pointed and dropped back on his red belly.

"Lightmark," he breathed. "Been to . . . Lightmark."

In the clear morning light of Pastora there were suddenly dark dreads without form, terrors out of imagination to make Magus shudder.

In the air Maya drew the sign against the evil eye.

IV

HANS HUYGENS died at dusk, propped against an ocher log in the little wooded hollow where Robin Dragonard made his camp.

Before he died the branded freebooter told them pieces of a tale which alternately excited Magus with a lust for wealth and chilled him with a superstitious fear.

Soon after the freebooter revealed that he'd been to Lightmark with the stolen skysled, Robin and Magus carried Huygens the short distance to Robin's camp. They settled the dying man as comfortably as possible. Maya saw to the careful removal of strips of the blue garment. A shard of skysled metal, snapped free from some interior frame, had driven into Huygen's midsection like a spear. Magus wouldn't risk trying to pull it out.

He went instead to fetch his pack. In its very bottom he carried some metallic paper packets containing analgesic salve. The salve eased Huygen's pain considerably.

The fat outlaw remained dazed. He babbled appreciation for Magus' help. He told them in big blubbery wheezes that he was sure he would be up and well soon.

Hearing this for the second or third time, Maya left his side abruptly. She turned away and covered her face with her hands. Magus stared at the tips of his boots.

Later Maya brewed a little broth from Robin's supplies. She fed it to Huygens in a cracked bowl. Then Magus sat down beside the man, unable to conceal his interest any longer.

"Can you tell us about Lightmark?"

Huygens licked a last dollop of broth from his upper lip. When he spoke, it was not in clear sentences but rather in groups of words punctuated by heavy breaths:

"I . . . saw the towers first when I put down. Went around the whole blasted planet once and . . . came up on the towers last. Everything else . . . gone in the wars. But the towers stood. Shining-bright, they were. Metal of some sort. Smooth . . . slim . . . and after I landed they . . . looked high as the sky. Hundreds of 'em bunched together. No gleam of rust. No mold-slop. Just bright . . . metal. Everything . . . else on that goddamned place was . . . waste. Desert. Hard land. Gone in the wars, whatever . . . living places there were. The . . . towers still stood."

"Hundreds, you say," Magus prompted. "Together. A city?"

"Or the headquarters of one of the commercial houses?" asked Robin.

Magus' quick glance said, *Then you've heard it too. Heard that one of the greatest of the corporations had its home on Lightmark but the war destroyed—*

"Don't think it's not the truth!" The sudden wheeze from Huygens seized Magus' attention again. "I can prove I was there. I went . . . into the place. Walked the . . . streets under the towers. Went inside what buildings I could get into . . . strange, awful damn places. Shiny metal. Cold. Everywhere. Machines. Trinkets, lying on benches in long rooms where people must've . . . worked once. I can prove I was there, I tell you. I brought back a . . . whole trunk full of junk.''

Magus' eyes were wide open. ''Where's the trunk now? In the skysled?''

''Yes, if . . . it's not smashed.''

''What things did you bring back?'' Robin whispered.

The obese man blinked sadly. Noon was already long past. The light of Graphos slanted low on the countryside. Somewhere a peasant hallooed. A dog barked in response.

''Trinkets,'' Huygens repeated. ''Junk. Gimcracks. Magical pieces. They must be magical pieces because some gave off . . . funny noises when I pressed little buttons.'' A tear. Another. Huygens' eyes were watering with exhaustion. ''I don't read or write any. I don't have the head to know what they were. I just figured they'd be . . . worth a lot on Pastora. I . . . was loading them into my old leather trunk when—''

A crawling shudder shook all of his flab and brought fresh blood to the surface of the rag bandage. Maya had wrapped around his middle.

''*They* came.''

''Who?'' Magus asked.

Huygens didn't hear. ''They came creepin' on me when . . . I was in one of the buildings.''

Robin craned forward. ''These were *people*? On Lightmark?''

''Uhh,'' Huygens said, meaning the negative. He

coughed hard. "Awful things. Awful. Tall and bony with sort of a . . . lizard-plate skin. Human-shaped as we. But . . . that's all. They wore these little kilts about their middles and . . . the one or two women had breasts, a figure, but this . . . lizard-skin was all over 'em. Their ears were long. Sharp. Their eyes . . . goddamn big. Whitish. Stuck out like balls on their foreheads . . . black centers big as my fist." He demonstrated with bloody fingers. "They spoke to me."

Maya's turn to be startled. "In your . . . our own language?"

"Very same, girl. They live in the rock hills 'round that place, they told me. Call themselves . . . the Brothers. They ride animals, too. Big ugly long-necked ones. With forked tails an' hairy foot-pads and . . . heads as big as the cathedral bell in New Cologne, yes. The Brothers said they'd lived on Lightmark forever. That the metal towers were holy or haunted or . . . something. Said it was the Brothers' job to keep men like me away. They recognized that maybe my kind and theirs were related, they . . . saw that much. Understood my speech. So maybe whatever spirits changed the sheep on Pastora to giants changed the Lightmark people too. . . ."

"Spirits, Huygens?" said Magus, really questioning himself. "Or did the rain from the wars do all that?"

"Same thing, all . . . magic. They took me out to the one who led them. No . . . different than the rest but for this . . . funny roostery crest dividing his head in half, from where his hair ought to start, back to the bottom of his neck. They called him Plume. Brother . . . Plume. He said I had to be punished. Punished in the Haunt-place."

Wind rustled trees at the clearing's edge. Magus kept his voice low. "Where was that?"

Sweat built up on Huygens' cheeks, foul-smelling and greasy.

"I can't . . . say. Inside my head maybe. A cave maybe. They hit my head a lot first. I went out . . . woke up there. Ah, I'm not a religious man but blessed God—"

He clutched Magus' arm and stared. Magus saw near-madness in his eyes.

"I was never in that . . . kind of place before. Countrysides such as no man in his right mind ever saw. Orange cliffs. Purple grass an' a yellow ocean. Plants . . . six times higher than me, asking . . . my name. And one minute the sky was a green and next it was copper and on and on changing . . . all the time, everything . . . changing. There were animals too. Balls of jelly. Whole things nothing but slimy arms. Something like a dappled black and white elephant with four tusks on either side of its head and . . . the noise! The noise near to cracked my skull, the plants whispering, the animals honking and . . . growling and . . . shaking everything as they . . . come after me and . . . the colors changing all the while. I ran, I ran. I ran from one animal, then another. I kept away from 'em somehow, they never . . . caught me. But I ran screaming, I'll tell you . . . that. Then all at once when the dapple elephant with eight tusks was on me, I fainted dead away."

Magus gave Robin a glance asking, *the truth?*

Robin looked puzzled. He shrugged. Magus continued questioning in a quiet voice:

"What happened when you woke up?"

"I was . . . back with them in one of the towers.

With the Brothers. I said where was that place, the Hauntplace? They . . . wouldn't tell me. On Lightmark? Off Lightmark? No, they never told. They just kept saying it was the . . . Lightmark land where the demons dwelled. Their words. The Lightmark land where the . . . demons dwelled. Even that nasty high cockalorum Brother Plume, he shook when he spoke about it." Huygens was crying. "I . . . may have been crazy for a time. No real place could . . . be that way. If it was . . . better a man be mad than go there."

Night came on.

After another cup of broth and a bit of saltmeat, Huygens finished his story. When the Brothers gathered to confer about him, Huygens managed to get hold of his leather trunk and dart away. Keeping to the shadows, he eluded the strange creatures.

Or perhaps they had wanted him to escape, deciding he had been sufficiently punished for setting foot in their holy, haunted city.

Huygens ran ten leagues to his skysled. He spent the journey back to Pastora drinking himself sodden under the control canopy. Control failure on reentry. And crash.

The freebooter dozed off. Robin had built a small shielded fire of log chips. The ocher flames etched Magus' face into a savage study. Maya finally asked him: "What are you thinking?"

"I'm thinking that if I could loot some of the trinkets of Lightmark, I could sell them on Pastora and be a rich man and all my problems would be gone. I'd retire—"

"You couldn't sell them with the authorities watching," Robin said.

Magus fingered his beard. "There are other ways."

"But the demons live on Lightmark, Father." Maya's violet eyes were fearful.

"Or lonely people changed by the war rains?" Robin murmured. "Changed the way the animals were changed here on Pastora?"

Magus half smiled. "Who knows? My head says don't believe in demons. My belly tells me they're real. But I was born and raised on Pastora, after all."

Hauntplace. It tormented him with its musical sound. Hauntplace.

Could he face that, whatever it might be? And live to loot more successfully than Huygens? His bowels grew taut. His forehead ached. He was afraid.

Hauntplace . . .

"I'm . . . dying, isn't that it?"

The voice pulled Magus around. Maya glanced up from scrubbing a cracked bowl with a blue leaf. Huygens had been asleep. Now he was awake, looking more lucid than he had all day. Magus said nothing. Robin studied the embers. Huygens quirked up the corners of his mouth.

"All at once, here, I came awake. Really awake. I know I'm all done. I can feel it inside me. The medication did no good. Couldn't help, could it?" Suddenly Huygens' cheeks streamed with tears. "Will you hold my hand, girl?"

Maya ran to him, crying herself. She knelt and clasped both his pitifully fat hands between her own slim ones. Huygens finally controlled himself.

"You've helped me, all of you. I wish I had something fine to give. All I have is the trunk in the sled. Take it if it's still in one piece. Take it and sell the accursed goddamned junk in it . . . the magical things.

I wish I'd never gone up there for the Lightmark magical things, I—''

A brilliant crimson bubble appeared on his lips. It burst. His head sagged forward.

Maya drew her hands away and stood up.

The moons were high. By their light they buried him, using an old trenching tool Robin provided. Then they went back to the skysled.

The metal had cooled. Magus wriggled in and out of the maze of wreckage until he found the small leathern trunk. It was square, with rope-twist carrying handles at either end. It had survived the crash with one corner knocked in.

Robin helped Magus drag it out and smash the fastening with a rock. Magus threw back the lid and quickly walked away.

Moonlight touched the peculiar objects inside.

A small black metal box with studs.

A larger, rectangular box with undecipherable yellow glyphs on it.

Some large spools that gleamed like chromium.

A chromium sphere with an iris arrangement set in one side.

A sheaf of rotting diagrams which Magus couldn't understand no matter what angle he viewed them from.

Faintly ashamed of himself, Magus felt his spine and palms itching. The chromium sphere and spools shone cold in the moonlight. Maya slipped her arm around him.

''Magical things.'' She was frightened too.

''I wonder,'' Magus breathed. ''Old Phlebos told me once that the truly magical things of this world were called pieces of scientific apparatus. Great thinkers used them before the nuclear rains. Phlebos maintained they weren't magic if you understood them. And he said they were made of metal.''

He drew away from Maya, finally working up enough courage to pick up one of the chromium spools. It felt smooth, chilly against his flesh.

Be a man! he said to himself. *Stop shivering inside!*

But he understood enough false magic to realize how little he knew of what might be the real kind. The spool he held terrified him deep to the bottom of his guts.

''Will they be of any use to us?'' Robin asked.

''Uncertain,'' was Magus' reply. ''But I won't leave them. Nor could I. Not after that poor old pirate gave them to us one breath this side of the grave.''

''They may be tainted by the Lightmark demons, Father,'' Maya warned.

''Or we may be cursed and damned to fear them because of our own ignorance. Hurry, now. Dark's best for traveling. We've been lucky with no pursuit today. Let's not push that luck, eh?''

Lugging the magical truck under the moons, Magus, Maya and Robin took the road to New Brussels.

V

"Aннн!" went the single sighing voice of the crowd. "*Ahhhhh!*"

A tiny iridescent ball of whitish-green fire blazed to life. It whirled and sputtered at the tip of the raised index finger of the right hand of Magus Blacklaw. A flamboyant figure in his shimmering black iricloth robe and scarlet sash with its silver embroidery of cabalistic symbols, he flashed his smile like a piece of merchandise and boomed his voice out over the motley little mob:

"Fate, my noble friends, brings many a surprise!"

Up went his third finger. *Pop!* A little green fireball joined the one already dazzling at the end of his index finger.

"—many a sudden turn of events—"

Out shot his ring finger. *Pop!* Now a trio of fireballs danced.

"—to blind and bedazzle the simple man!"

Pop! Pop! A fourth and fifth fireball glared on the tips of his little finger and thumb.

Magus stood on the flat bed of a rented carter's wagon under the gargoyle shadow of the cathedral of

New Brussels. Sweaty faces with white eyes turned up to him. He, however, kept his eye on one particular person in his audience.

The portly woman had rich apparel and an appalling face. She also had the unmistakable look of one who had suddenly found a solution for her problem, be it financial or—God save the man nuzzled by that faintly moustached upper lip!—marital. Magus had found his profit for the night.

He played to the woman, manipulating his hand so that the five little fireballs began to weave an intricate pattern, whirling around one another like tiny planets.

Gayly dressed in an orange smock that echoed the flaring color of two torches socketed into the wagon's bed, Maya slipped up behind him. Magus had only to hold out his left hand and the big ebony silk was there. It billowed in the night wind that blew across the immense square.

The square was dark except for a smear of light from a distant inn-yard and the torches burning on the wagon.

Magus wove the fireballs in the air for another moment. Then he cried: "Good folk! The bedazzlements of sudden ill fortune can spin the mind just as these little lights spin before your eyes!"

The fireballs shot round and round as Magus writhed his hand like a plastic, boneless thing. "In such a state, confusion can lead a man . . . or woman . . ." That was quick interpolation directed at the matron in fine clothes. Splendid! She was already fingering her cloth-of-gold carrybag.

"Confusion can lead a man or woman to the wrong act, the ill-conceived choice unless—unless a superior power such as an oracle or other person suitably versed in the occult viewing of the future is called upon, at modest fee, by the tormented victim. In this fortuitous circumstance it is the work of but a moment for the wizard's far-seeing mind to analyze the choices and, calling upon his arcane talents to drive out, exorcise and otherwise eliminate the evil confusion—"

Round and round over his head Magus whipped the voluminous black silk with his left hand. His voice rose almost to a chant. "—forever, forever, as if they never existed!"

Down whipped the silk covering the fireballs dancing on his fingertips. He crushed the silk onto his right hand, then ripped it away.

"Ahhhhhhhh!"

Grinning, Magus held up his right hand.

The fireballs were gone.

What claptrap, he said to himself. *Yet how they do swallow it*.

His eyes flickered beyond the crowd to the paved emptiness of the great square. To his left loomed the cathedral, a secular structure despite its name. Stone gargoyles peered down from its heights. He could see no authorities, the pikearmed toughs with light metal helmets patrolling on nightwatch. At the inn across the square men loudly sang a dirty song. Otherwise it was quiet.

On this, his third night in New Brussels, Magus was beginning to feel more or less secure.

The crowd applauded the end of the performance and broke up. Maya jumped from the wagon, carrying a silk among the peasants. One or two threw in a ha'credit. Maya gave them a sweet smile in return. But this wasn't the reward Magus was after. He still had his eyes on the portly matron. She was hesitating, fingering her purse. She hadn't left. He announced loudly:

"Private consultations are available at special fee for any interested."

The others drifted into the dark, laughing nervously as they discussed the half hour of vanishings, mentalism and hand magic they'd just witnessed. The matron waddled forward. Magus leaped from the wagon and landed lightly beside her. Fresh oil on his beard made it glisten. His teeth blazed in the torchflare. The matron turned pink in the face.

"You wish a consultation, Madam?"

"If the cost is not too high." She showed nervousness in a simper.

"I shall set the fee lower than usual because of your exceeding charm, dear lady." Magus continued to grin. A few paces away, Maya giggled behind her hand.

"Thank you wizard."

"What is the nature of your problem?"

The matron crowded in close, bathing Magus in her clove scent. "Most delicate and personal. I am afraid my husband has taken a young consort of the female sex. And all because, in past months, I have somehow lost my power to attract his favor and attentions."

"I find that hard to believe, dear lady. You are most—"

Suddenly his black brows hooked together. In the shadow just beyond the torchlight, Maya was frantically trying to attract his attention. Magus patted the matron's ringed hand.

"One moment please. Excuse me."

He stalked toward his daughter, his anger rising.

"This one can be plucked, you ninny," he hissed. "Don't disturb me when—"

"It's Robin, Father. There behind the wagon." Maya's violet eyes flooded with fear.

Magus whipped around. Robin leaned against one of the wagon's big wood wheels. In his new doublet hose and cheap cloak, he looked more or less civilized.

And drunk.

Robin weaved on his feet. His face was pale, sweat-dappled. Magus' eyes went down to slits. Blood stained Robin's right temple.

On the far side of the square by the lighted inn, armor clinked. Boots thudded. Peering into the dark, Magus saw the flash of light metal helmets.

Authorities! Half a dozen of them, charging across the square toward the wagon. Other darker figures hurried along behind.

"Fetch my sword from under the wagon, Maya."

Magus hauled one torch from its socket and dashed it dark on the paving. He extinguished the second one and then ran around to Robin. The young man's gold eyes were bleary.

Magus sniffed. "Drinking. And you got in a fight? I gave you leave to have a meal and a cup while we worked, Robin, but I didn't give you leave to go brawling."

"I—I'm sorry. The wine was too damn strong. Four cups and all at once I was sitting in that inn over there, bragging about you. Only because you and Maya are my friends!"

Bootfalls and halloos sounded from the center of the square. "Who started the brawl, boy?"

"Men sitting back in a corner. Didn't see them until too late."

Magus stared out over the square. Behind the metal-helmeted authorities the blacker figures came on. Swirling, formless figures in—*robes*.

Magus' belly turned stone-heavy. His fingers bit into Robin's forearm. "You mean those men running behind the authorities?"

"Y-yes. In long brown robes and sandals. I swear I didn't mean to drink so much."

"Maya!" Magus looked savage now. "Take this poor sot and run as best you can. I'll try to draw them off another way. We'll meet back at the inn where we've put our things. Don't worry about me until dawn at least. Thanks to our young friend I may have a very long night in store."

The running men had only a quarter of the huge square left to cross. Magus shoved Maya and Robin away and closed his fingers around the hilt of his sword. Robin stumbled and mumbled as the girl dragged him toward the shadows surrounding a closed-down sweet booth. They vanished.

Even the matron had fled. Magus was alone. He tucked his robe up into the scarlet sash so he wouldn't trip on the hem. Then, slipping to the left, he started on the run toward the dark along the front portico of the cathedral.

"Hold up, magician. By authority of the bailiff of New Delft you are commanded to stop!"

The pursuit had arrived. And Robin had got clackingly sodden at the wrong time in the wrong place, and probably blared the name Blacklaw too loudly once too often. *Well, I should have known better than to believe the authorities of New Delft would give up the chase.*

Once more the command to stop rang out behind.

"See you in hell!" *Magus yelled back. And up the cathedral steps he went, three at a time.*

The cathedral housed the bureaucracy of the High Governors of the province. His plan was to get inside if at all possible, loot a deserted office of an official uniform of authority—a brown belted robe of coarse cloth—and use this as a disguise to elude further pursuit. He banged up to the top of the steps. A thrown pike sailed at him from behind. He ducked. The pike struck sparks from the portico pillar inches from his head.

He looked right and left. The left way seemed darkest.

Helms flashing, the authorities poured up the steps behind him. Another pike sailed, missed, clanged. Magus plunged down the side stone porch. At the far end cresset-lamps glimmered at an entranceway.

He ran harder. His chest began to ache.

Curses, yells, pike-clangs created an uproar behind him. Magus was halfway to the flickering door light when two men erupted from a niche to his right. From their obesity and their monks' robes he recognized local bureaucrats.

"Stand, you!" one of the bureaucrats bellowed, hauling out his sword with effort. In a second Magus found himself cutting and parrying, *cling-ping*, trying to hack his way past.

He dodged as the fatter of the two puffed and drove a thrust at his guts. He flung himself back against a pillar. The thin blade whistled past his neck. He chopped down with his free arm. The bureaucrat cried out. Magus hammered the flab at the back of the man's neck twice more. The bureaucrat tumbled.

Robes swirling, the second bureaucrat leaped over

the fallen man. He brandished both a sword and a dagger. Magus shot his right arm in beneath the other's sword. His point sank into robe-cloth and flesh beneath. The bureaucrat squealed and thrashed his arms, raking the air wildly with his dagger. Magus backed off, got his boots tangled in the habit of the one who'd fallen.

Off balance, Magus tasted the bile of panic in his mouth. The dagger bit a hunk out of his left cheek. The pain blazed through him like a sudden fever. He toppled back against the authorities and the bailiff's men from New Delft.

Magus kicked, punched, writhed. Useless. The authorities used the butts of their pikes to bludgeon him down.

He crawled up on hands and knees. Out past the pillars the great square of the drowsing city was empty of people. A snatch of dirty song drifted from the inn. Magus thought briefly of Maya and Robin. Got away, did they? That was some small good—

The authorities bludgeoned him again.

And once again.

And several more times.

His head burst with intense light and he slid out against the cool stone of the porch, senseless.

A massive gavel knocked. It made a sepulchral sound in the immense chamber whose walls were lost to sight, off there beyond the huddled ranks of monkish men.

High overhead a series of three brilliant stained-glass windows let in a few feeble shafts of sun. But they scattered their light long before they drifted down to the murk of the lower part of the cathedral hall. Moldering tapestries gleamed here and there. In the reverent hush a rich voice rolled forth.

"By request of the assembled assistant bailiffs of our sister city of New Delft, the Cathedral Tribune here convened does open the formal charging of the accused, Magus Blacklaw, place of habitation unknown."

Though he knew the setting was trumpery, the foggy, echoing stillness of the place terrified Magus Blacklaw a little. He stood in a dock that soared thirty feet above the damp stone floor. Higher still, on another platform, the three members of the Tribune, ancient bureaucrats in brown robes and skullcaps, sat surveying him with liverish eyes.

Magus had been wakened just before they dragged him in here. His iricloth robe and scarlet sash seemed cheap and shabby to him now. A dressing had been slapped over the wound on his cheek. He took hold of the edges of the dock as the central of the three members of the Cathedral Tribune called for the city's prosecutor.

The prosecutor was a feral, thin-shanked fellow who strutted in black silk. He wore a gold amulet on a chain around his neck, and carried a book-roll.

"What is the charge to be heard, prosecutor?" said the man on the high platform.

"By request of the bailiff of New Delft, your worship, it is threefold. Firstly, claiming powers reserved to the High Governors of Pastora. Secondly, thereby impersonating a true wizard or manipulator of the magical apparatus which has been the property of the state since before the nuclear rains. Thirdly, using said falsely claimed powers for financial gain at the expense of citizens. So requests the bailiff of New Delft. After suitable study''—a foxy glance up at Magus, who gripped the dock rail with white hands; the prosecutor brandished his book-roll—''the duly constituted prosecutor's office of New Brussels fully concurs with the charges.''

''What punishment is requested if the defendant is found guilty?'' asked another member of the Tribune.

Magus' palms sweated against the wood of the dock rail. This was very bad. The prosecutor replied:

''The punishment requested is death by decapitation.''

''You damned pack of frauds!'' Magus roared, leaning far forward out of the dock. ''You keep all the working machines for yourselves, your sleds and your meccanodogs, but do you understand them? No! But that's quite all right, isn't it, as long as the poor slime you rule—your dear stinking citizens—*think* you understand them! And you very neatly suppress the idea that anyone else *could* understand them, and so you keep yourselves in office, and sit on your hoggish rear ends like—''

''Cease!'' cried the old man in the center of the high platform. His voice was surprisingly loud. ''Remember where you are.''

''I know all too—''

''*Silence!*''

The prosecutor strutted to the base of the dock. He rapped for Magus' attention. Magus looked down, breathing hard and regretting the burst of temper. But he wouldn't crawl for them. Let them have his head. Things could certainly get no worse.

"Is it your contention, wizard," asked the prosecutor with particularly hasty emphasis on the last word, "that you possess the secrets of manipulating magical apparatus? Secrets reserved to the High Governors by all civil as well as natural laws?"

"That is my contention," Magus lied, without quite knowing why.

"You contend you are a true wizard, not a false one?"

"Yes, you strutting eunuch, I do!"

The prosecutor squealed as though gored. *Well,* thought Magus, *now you've done it.*

But he gained a certain satisfaction from his impromptu lie. Out in the mists the robed bureaucrats stirred, whispering and whispering. With effort Magus put on a smug face.

"This insolence . . .!"

The prosecutor paused to bring himself under control with several deep breaths. Then:

"We request immediate hearing and sentence, rather than observance of the formal day of delay. For the good of all our citizens, such blasphemies must be dealt with swiftly."

The Cathedral Tribune concurred to a man. The trial lasted less than half an hour.

Three assistant bailiffs from New Delft testified via statements read from book-rolls. They described Magus' trickery in the town from which he had fled. The destruction of the meccanodogs was also presented as evidence by a huntsman. Magus was not allowed to speak in his own defense. The prosecutor harangued for ten minutes on reasons why he should be found gulity.

He was.

The Cathedral Tribune pronounced sentence in unison. The bureaucrats applauded.

Authorities hustled Magus from the dock. They took him down to a dungeon five levels beneath the cathedral. There he was given some soggy onion bread, a jar of thin wine, a sour pot as a sop to sanitation, and instructions to await the execution, which might come at any moment.

VI

A LITTLE ORANGE FLAME danced in a bowl of scented oil, high up in a niche in the cell's sweating stone wall. The cell measured about six by six by eight feet high. Magus promptly explored every cranny and concluded that the mortaring between the blocks was hopelessly sound.

He sprawled in a corner on musty straw. He sipped at the wine and tried to purge his mind of the thought that the door—a heavy, smooth gray plastic, obviously newer than the rest of the place—might open at any moment to reveal a headsman.

Lying there, Magus conceived several plans of escape and rejected each. Not a one was practical. All required throttling of one or more of his guards. Do that and his freedom would be worthless even if he gained it. They'd hound him from one end of Pastora to another.

Escape by violence was to be avoided. That left escape by his wits, which seemed to have failed him temporarily.

If he could only convince his captors that his assertions in the dock were the truth! He suspected that the

High Governors and their toadying bureaucrats and authorities knew as little of the internal workings of such things as skysleds as he did. They simply pretended to know, and had the authority to enforce the pretense.

A tantalizing possibility occurred to him. He stared at the lamp flame and sloshed the wine jar to and fro, thinking.

A good idea? Yes, a splendid idea! But how to bring it off? It would take powers of a genuine magician to get what he needed down into this hole. And even then there was no guarantee the scheme would work. Or that he could go through with it. With a shudder he remembered the feel of the chromium spool against his hand.

The motorized latch whined in the smooth gray door.

Startled, Magus dropped the wine jar. It smashed and dripped red wine on the straw. He jumped up, arranged his stained iricloth robe and lifted his chin arrogantly as the door swung open, doubtless to reveal his executioner.

A dirty-jowled authority in metal helm stood outside. He barred the entrance to someone Magus couldn't see. To this unseen person the authority croaked:

"It's a nice sum and all. The spirits know I need it. But keep your voice down when you're inside. If you're discovered and you try to drag me into it, I'll deny knowing you until the three moons fall out of the sky. Five minutes is all. They'll be back from the nutrient mess in about five minutes. I'll rap when it's time. You come out then or you won't get led back out. That clear?"

"Clear. Now stand out of my way," said Robin Dragonard, appearing suddenly in the opening.

The authority stepped back, eyeing the proceedings with greedy uncertainty. Under his left arm Robin carried Hans Huygens' small trunk. He came in quickly, dropped the trunk. The authority touched a control in the corridor wall. The smooth door shut with a formidable chunk.

Robin's gold eyes met those of the older man, worried.

Magus grinned suddenly. Robin didn't know what to make of it.

"Since I got you into this," Robin said, "I thought you might go for my throat."

"How could I?" Magus chuckled. He pointed at the trunk. "You brought that. Are you a secret mentalist?"

Robin sniffed the sour cell. "What do you mean?"

"I decided that infernal trunk was all that could save my head. For the better part of an hour I've been going over and over ways to get it in here. All impossible."

Robin shrugged a bit sheepishly. "There's no magic in it, Magus. It's not even high noon yet and the news of what happened at the trial is all over the city. The people are preparing for a real celebration at the beheading tomorrow—"

"Tomorrow! You have more information than I."

"It's said one of the members of the Tribune has to be absent from the city this afternoon."

"Then that explains it. A fortunate delay. I'll have time with—that." He nodded toward the trunk.

Magus wasn't quite sure he wanted to open the thing again. He scored himself for being childish. This was no time to let superstitious tradition turn his guts to water. Robin spoke again:

When I heard what happened, I blamed myself."

"Damn well you should." Magus' smile relieved

the sting of the words. "But accidents, even fool ones, are forgivable. Especially since you brought the trunk. Is Maya all right?"

"Yes, she's safe," Robin replied. "Hiding at the inn. It was she who suggested I take the earnings from the performances and try to bribe my way into the dungeon. I was surprised at how easy that part was. These pigs—" Robin gathered spit in his mouth and blew it out. "Rotten. Venal. They twitch when they smell a few illegal ha'credits. I was the one who thought of the trunk, though. I heard that at the trial you said you were a true wizard after the prosecutor said otherwise. It occurred to me that if you would find a way to use any of the apparatus in the trunk"—an uncertain gesture—"if they're not too old, or beyond comprehension . . . you might convince the authorities that you were telling the truth. I could try to help you escape some other way. But I think that would be foolish. If nothing else works, Maya and I will try to rescue you at the beheading. It's to be held in the public square. But an escape like that will only mean pursuit—"

"Forever and forever." Magus gave a quick nod. "Robin, I compliment you for having more wits that I credited you with at first. Your reasoning paralleled mine exactly. This trunk is the only way out of here save by bloodshed. We'll save that for a last resort."

Robin nodded slowly. "The Dragonards may drink too much. But we've never been called dull. I wanted you to know that."

"I do, I do." Magus murmured, dropping to his knees beside the trunk. He was anxious to get at its contents.

"I also came here for Maya's sake."

"That's good, Robin. That's fine." Magus reached for the hemp-twist trunk handles.

Abruptly Robin seized his shoulder and jerked him to his feet. "Damn you, magician, pay attention to me! I'm responsible for your sentence! I expect—"

"You expect me to coddle you like a forgiving father, is that it?" Magus snarled. "Well, there's no time."

"I expect you to treat me like a man! If you doubt I am . . ." Robin's hand dropped toward the hilt of his sword.

Magus blinked. He made a swift finger-to-mouth gesture signaling the need for silence. Robin's eyebrows shot up as he remembered. He flushed but he didn't let go of his sword.

The two men stared at each other a moment longer. It was Magus who broke the tension with a grin.

"All right, enough! I'll treat you as what you are, Robin. A clever man. A brave one. I never meant to patronize you."

Robin's gold eyes were deadly. "I've killed men protecting my flock."

"I believe you."

Suddenly Magus was conscious of a new, deeper understanding between them. An equality. No longer was Robin merely a loutish lad who'd gotten him into this situation. He was a fighting friend. Completely on Magus' side. The moment ripened, and Magus found himself wondering whether Maya saw Robin's admirable qualities.

A light fist knocked on the door. Again. The door swung inward. Lamplight flashed on the metal helm of the authority.

"I hear them singing on the way back from mess. We go now or not at all."

"Luck," Robin called, and ducked out the door.

The authority touched the hidden control. The door swung. Just before he was shut from sight, the authority eyed the small trunk and made the sign against evil eye. Sweat shone in the pores of his pitted cheeks.

Silence. Magus was alone in the clammy cell with the trunk. He took a deep breath and with one kick of a jackboot knocked the lid open.

There they gleamed, fearful puzzles. The square metal box with studs. The larger box covered with yellow glyphs. The chromium sphere with its iris device on one side. The empty chromium spools, the rotting diagrams.

Frightful demon-instruments? Or only seeming demonic because he, like any citizen of Pastora, had been bred to fear them?

Old Phlebos called them scientific apparatus. Of what sort, then? What magic did they perform? Could they have been wrought well enough to retain their powers for years? It seemed a slim chance. And yet the skysleds had endured since the time of the nuclear rains. . . .

The orange candle sputtered. On his knees beside the truck, Magus lifted out the chromium sphere.

He studied the one bright yellow stud discovered on the bottom. He wished he were a religious man. His hands shook. Carefully, carefully, he held the sphere in one hand and pressed the bright yellow stud with the finger of the other.

The iris went *snaap!* Within the sphere a whirring began.

Face slicked with sweat, Magus laughed sharply and fell to hauling the other things from the trunk.

By the end of the night, for the first time in his cynical life, he knew how it felt to be a wizard with the authentic powers of antiquity alive in his hands.

VII

THE GOLD AMULET on the chain around the prosecutor's neck glared like a baleful eye as it caught sun falling down through the stained glass overhead. With a furious glance at Magus in the dock, the prosecutor said to the Tribune:

"May I state into the record that my office is unalterably opposed to this cheap charade. We demand that the guilty man be taken forthwith to the block constructed in the square outside. We demand that sentence be carried out immediately. To allow this mountebank to make fools of us—as he will surely do if we entertain his pathetic professions of powers he could not possibly possess—"

The oldest of the skullcapped bureaucrats on the high platform rapped the massive gavel.

"Your objection is noted, prosecutor. We need no instruction concerning our wisdom or folly. The guilty man is entitled to prove his statement that he is a true wizard if he can do so." The whey cheeks sucked in briefly as the old man in the brown robe drew a whistling breath. His old eyes, rheum-watered at the corners, peered down at Magus with unusual intensity. "Indeed we shall be most interested if he can do so."

Magus shifted his position in the dock. His right boot bumped the corner of the trunk. He'd overcome his fear of its contents during the long night of trial and error. He still did not understand the reason or reasons underlying the effect the pieces of apparatus could produce. But his concern was of a different sort now.

If something within the objects failed, if the effect that he had produced several times before dawn in his cell could not be produced one more time, he was finished.

With effort he banished the thought. He turned his gaze out over the crowd jammed into the hall. Hundreds of faces turned up toward him in the damp, uncertain light.

The Cathedral Tribune had opened the main doors to allow the public to witness the demonstration. The authority bringing Magus up from the dungeon had commented that the Tribune could hardly have done otherwise. Word of Magus' request had spread outside the building immediately after first light. Even before the Tribune had acceded to his request a mob had gathered. People wanted to see the man who dared to stand up and call himself a true wizard. Magus wiped damp palms on his robe as the central member of the Tribune called down:

"Let the proceedings begin. The clerks shall take extra precautions to note each detail, however trivial, into the official book-rolls. Wizard, you contend that you possess the true powers?"

Magus swallowed hard. Were Maya and Robin out in the crowd? His voice was surprisingly forceful as he answered: "Yes, I do."

"What evidence do you offer to support your statement?"

Magus reached down. He lifted the trunk and set it on the rail of the dock. A peasant woman in a fusty shawl shrank back shuddering at the base of the dock. The prosecutor posed haughtily, awaiting the first mistake.

"Firstly," said Magus, "I offer this. My trunk of magic devices. I did not have it in my possession when I was arrested. Nor did I have it when placed in the dungeon. This morning, however, when I knocked on my cell door and made my request for this hearing, the trunk was in my hands."

"Several of the authorities have so attested," said another member of the Tribune.

"How did you come into the possession of the trunk while locked in your cell?" asked the third.

"By exercising my powers," Magus lied. Could they be fooled for an instant? Only if he were less frightened of real magic than they. He had to keep remembering that. "I transported the trunk from its previous location, through the solid stone walls of this cathedral, into my cell."

"Based upon the evidence that you indeed appeared to have done just this," responded the central member of the Tribune, "we made our decision to allow you to appear before us. Proceed, Magus Blacklaw."

A flurry of signs against evil eye out in the crowd. Magus opened the trunk. A tall man down there with the rabble watched him with a searing concentration. The man had a long, pale face beneath the cowl of his cloak, and shaggy bright red eyebrows and dropping moustache. As Magus opened the trunk, the prosecutor began a whining harangue:

"—submit that the story is a lie! An accomplice fetched the trunk into his cell last night."

One of the Tribune members pursed his lips. "Exactly how, prosecutor?"

"Bribery, of course! One or more authorities were paid to—"

"Do you have proof to support that statement?"

The prosecutor turned scarlet. "No. But given sufficient time—"

"Then be silent. Magus Blacklaw, be so good as to continue."

What was wrong? Magus wondered as he pushed back the trunk lid and took out the chromium sphere. The crowd whispered, drew back. The members of the Tribune actually seemed to be favoring him now. Taking his side against the prosecutor. Why?

With his right hand he lifted the chromium sphere high over his head.

"This is one of the magical devices I shall employ to prove my contention. I shall point it toward your Excellencies. It will make a strange noise. But I promise you no harm will come to you."

"No doubt he hired some craftsman to put that thing together for him," the prosecutor exclaimed.

Magus thrust the chromium sphere downward. "Then handle it yourself."

"No! Ah, that is, I do not deem it necessary—"

Magus wanted to laugh. *Fear!* he thought. *Fear's made them all cowards. Fear of the past. Of the truth. It's exactly as old Phlebos said.*

One member of the Tribune leaned forward. "Prosecutor! Bring the object up to us so that we may examine it for ourselves."

The prosecutor went white. He reached up. Magus dropped the sphere into his outstretched hands.

The man actually writhed at the contact. There was a ripple of snickering in the crowd. The prosecutor was too petrified to be angry. He stumbled toward the steep, narrow stairs which led up one side of the high platform. He juggled the sphere gingerly by cupping both his palms, causing the central member of the Tribune to say:

"And have a care, prosecutor, that you do not drop the magical device in an attempt to ruin it and discredit the wizard."

Wizard? Magus thought. *It's almost as if they want to believe in me.* From somewhere outside the great building came the hammer-hammer of the carpenters finishing the headsman's block.

Perhaps determined not to imitate the prosecutor's craven performance, the Tribune members passed the sphere back and forth among themselves with no hesitation. Finally the prosecutor brought the sphere down the stairs again. With visible relief he handed it back to Magus. The crowd was dead silent.

From the Tribune: "We concur that the object, outwardly at least, has all the characteristics of a magical device, including lightness and metallic composition."

With a sage nod Magus raised the sphere slowly over his head again. He took care that the iris-like device was angled upward toward the Tribune members. He added a few unnecessary but effective theatrics—closed eyes, wordless and soundless mumblings—as he reached beneath the sphere and touched the bright yellow stud. In the silence the hammers rapped sharp from the square.

Snaap! went the iris. The whirring began.

Magus continued holding the sphere aloft. After

several seconds he saw what he'd seen with such wonderment the first time in his cell. A microthin slot opened in the side of the sphere away from the iris.

A white edge appeared in the slot. This edge became a faintly sticky rectangle of white bordered plastic-like black stuff, a microthin sheet oozing slowly from the slot.

Magus caught the sheet in his free hand as it came all the way out of the sphere. The sticky coating burned a little, but previous contact with it had produced no ill effects.

From the trunk he scooped up the larger of the two black boxes, the one covered with weird yellow glyphs. After nine failures during the night, Magus had finally succeeded in discovering its use on the tenth try. A yellow glyph-arrow pointed to a slot at one end of the box.

With a flourish Magus slipped the sticky white-edged rectangle far enough into the slot so that it held. By trial and error he'd discovered the right sequence of studs to press on the side of the box. He was careful as he did it now.

He pressed the third stud from the left, top row. This produced a ratcheting sound from inside the box. The slot began to swallow the rectangle.

Magus pressed the stud directly below the first one. A thin whistling began.

Finally he pressed a lacquered blue, at the extreme right, bottom row.

The thin rectangle disappeared into the bowels of the box. Magus set the box on the dock rail. The waiting was the hellish part. The process took a minute or more.

The members of the Tribune whispered. Moon-face

peasants watched from the chamber floor. Their mouths hung open. Their eyes were big and round, their cheeks sweat-sliced.

"At this moment," Magus said, "forces within the device are at work to produce their magical effect."

"And just what is this effect?" the prosecutor helped. "Is it of any significance?"

Magus was ready for that. He'd pondered long on a name for the thing, the whatever-it-was that came out of the box.

"I have formed an image of the innermost personalities of the three learned Excellencies of the Tribune. The image is known as a picture of souls."

Picture of souls.

Like a grassfire it ran through the crowd. Even the prosecutor repeated it to himself as a tic jerked in his cheek. *Picture of souls.*

Magus was desperately conscious of the passage of time. He held his sweating hands tight on the black box, waiting, waiting for the slit to open at the other end.

The box had gone silent. Something was wrong!

No, he was only getting panicky. The delay was normal. It had happened before, when he finally created a dim image of the part of the wall at which the iris device had been pointed in his cell.

The microthin slit at the end of the box opened with a little syrupy gulp. The edge of the new rectangle appeared.

The rectangle's surface had somehow hardened within the box. Yet the rectangle itself remained flexible. Magus ripped it free of the slot. The tiny slot-teeth clashed as Magus held the rectangle up, looking at it against the stained glass overhead.

Black. Smeary. There was nothing—

Sweat in his eyes had blinded him. He shuddered as though coming out of a trance.

"The picture of your souls," he said in a hoarse voice, "is finished."

Upon the rectangle was etched an image of the heads and shoulders of the three members of the Tribune. Sunlight leaked through the blackened sheet, lighting up the tones of black and white that were mysteriously, inexplicably reversed. The dark wall behind the Tribune appeared white in the picture of souls. Their white cheeks and foreheads were the darkest areas of the image. Altogether it was a total reversal of reality, though there was no mistaking the accurate likenesses of the subjects. The purpose of the thing? Magus hadn't the faintest idea.

"The picture of souls, your Excellencies, is my proof that I possess the powers which I claimed."

"Hand up the picture of souls," ordered a Tribune member. "Prosecutor . . .?"

Once more the feral-faced man climbed the narrow stairs, holding the black sheet in one trembling hand. Magus gripped the dock rail tightly. The cowled man with the bristling red brows and moustaches was watching him closely. As the Tribune members passed the picture of souls from hand to hand, the stranger raised a fist and called:

"Excellencies! May a citizen address a question to the man in the dock?"

The central Tribune member scowled. "That is a citizen's right, provided the question is pertinent."

The man stepped forward. People in the crowd drew back, dismayed at his audacity. The man had a loping stride. He swallowed up whole yards of floor in one stretch of his long legs. The man's clothing was worn and colorless. A blade in a sword-harness swung at his waist. The harness too showed signs of considerable wear, indicating to Magus that the fellow might be some kind of wandering fighting man.

"I ask the wizard where he came by his magic paraphernalia." The man's eyes, a dull, hard gray, met and held his. "On the planet Lightmark, perhaps?"

A terrified murmur in the crowd. Who was the stranger? Some friend of Huygens' come sniffing after revenge? Magus kept his face immobile as he answered:

"My sources of power are known to me alone. They come from a level of knowledge far too high for the wits of common people to comprehend. Therefore—"

"That's gibberish! Give me a straight answer!"

The central Tribune member rapped his gavel. "Wizard, you are not obliged to answer a person of such obviously insignificant station." A glower at the moustached man. "Ruffianism will not be tolerated. Be warned."

"I will not answer," Magus said.

With a sullen shrug and a last keen glance at Magus, the stranger spun and melted back into the crowd.

The Cathedral Tribune deliberated only a few moments longer. The bent heads raised. The central member fixed Magus with a curiously friendly stare.

"We find this wizard speaks the truth. The charges are set aside, and the punishment likewise. Walk among us in perfect safety. You are a true wizard indeed." The gavel thundered three times.

Pandemonium. People surged forward to look up at Magus from below the dock. Magus grinned and tried to keep from passing out with sheer relief.

A moment later he heard a cry. "Father?"

There was Maya's lovely face, and Robin's, just below him. He waved.

The Cathedral Tribune watched as he collected his apparatus, shut his trunk and walked down out of the dock to freedom.

The inn sat on a side street near the cathedral square. It was called the Blind Pig. It had a cheerful common room, great platters of roast saltmeat, pewter tankards of ale, a blazing hearth and the conviviality of a friendly madhouse.

At sundown Magus, Maya and Robin retired to the hearth-side to eat and drink and celebrate. Since then the place had been packed. Sightseers came and went, ogling the wizard through the smoke. Swilling ale, Magus was having a grand time. He relished the attention, the laughter, the feel of the fire on the soles of his bootless feet, the smile in Maya's eyes as Robin refilled her tankard and managed to brush her hand while doing it.

Laughing, Maya said, "Father, you were magnificent. But weren't you terrified?"

"A wizard is never terrified."

"Where's your magic trunk, wizard?" Someone called from the back of the press.

"Locked in my room above stairs. And the first man or woman to go up those stairs gets this sword through the belly."

The crowd roared. A plump-breasted bargirl bent and kissed-whispered into his ear as she handed him a fresh tankard. He patted her hand. "Later, duckling, later. I—"

Cold wind blew on Magus' bare feet. Silence swept the smoky room like a swift plague.

Magus lunged for his sword-hilt. Drunk he missed. By that time the men in monks' robes had thrust through the crowd and surrounded him with a ring of pikes. Their heads were cowled. These were not authorities. These were bailiffs.

Across the way, Robin bent his hand toward his own blade, gold eyes wary in the glare of the hearth.

"Magus Blacklaw, you are summoned," said the bailiff in charge.

"What? I'm a free man! The Cathedral Tribune said—"

"That you were free? True. It's not questioned. We come on behalf of a greater power. You are called before the High Governors of Pastora."

The barmaid screamed.

Cold sober, Magus pulled on one boot, then the other. Was this the prosecutor striking back? Magus stood up. A hearth log fell, sparking.

"What's the purpose of the summons? Am I charged with another crime?"

Firelight reflections smoldered in the bailiff's eyes. "Not yet."

Abruptly Magus made his decision. "Damned if I will!" And he pulled steel.

The bailiff in charge barked, "Man or woman who aids him will be seized and beheaded before morning."

Magus backed toward the hearth. Robin got to his feet. The bailiffs reversed their pikes, holding them with butts forward. All at once the leader said: "Surround him and take him."

The bailiffs moved in, ramming their pike butts at Magus' head.

He dodged left. He thrust Maya from the bench where she sat. He seized the back of the bench, vaulted up and over.

Robin jumped to the hearth and thrust out with his sword at a charging bailiff. The man parried, turned Robin's blade aside, thrust the pike at his face. Frantically Robin slid backward. The pike tip tore bloody skin from the left side of his neck.

The other bailiffs swarmed around Magus, hacking at him with pike butts. He kicked a table over in their way. He snatched up a tankard and bashed another bailiff's cowl. The tankard crumpled and the bailiff collapsed.

Tapster and barmaid and citizen scattered, yelling and screaming, making it difficult for Magus to fight his way free. The bailiffs rushed him again. A pike butt slammed his temple. Another.

Cursing, Magus struck back. A fleeing citizen jarred his elbow as he thrust. The blade went crooked, stabbing into the bailiff's left ribs. The man shrieked and fell.

Instantly the tenor of the attack changed. Bailiff after bailiff swept his cowl back. They were lean-faced, deeply sunburned men. Hard. Capable. And now they were angered. They circled him with the killing ends of their pikes foremost.

The bailiff in charge came fighting his way through the crowd, shouting at his men: "Use the wooden end, damn you! He's to be taken alive!"

Obscene curses as the bailiffs obeyed, massed to move in again, shoulder butted to shoulder. Magus retreated. Past an overturned table. Suddenly Maya cried out.

Magus looked in her direction, saw her struggling with a bailiff while another fenced Robin. Blood ran into Robin's eyes from splotchy forehead wounds. Magus kept moving backward. All at once his back slammed into something hard.

He screwed his head around. He'd backed into one of the huge rocker-braced kegs of ale along the common room's outer wall. He slid to the right as the bailiffs charged.

He ducked his head to avoid the first pike blow. The pike missed him, striking a keg and smashing through a stave. Magus nearly drowned in cascades of pungent ale and foam.

The floor turned slippery. He skidded as they closed around him. The leader stormed to the center of the group as Magus was seized, his sword ripped from his fingers.

Shaking, the chief bailiff said, "If you've killed any of my men—" He gained control. "You're a stinking, filthy sight for the High Governors. Blind his eyes!"

Magus had a last glimpse of Maya bending over a fallen Robin on the far side of the room. The tavern was a wasteland of ruined furniture, spilled platters, splintered benches, overturned mugs. The smell of ale hung over everything.

The bailiffs wound a thick black silk round and round

his head. Magus was dazed, angry, desperately worried.

Why did the High Governors want him? Why?

Chilly night wind bathed his cheeks. They pushed him outside and the long, blind march through the night began.

VIII

A HAND TORE the blinding silk away. Magus blinked into a dazzle of lamps.

"We brought him here with some difficulty," said the leader of the bailiffs from somewhere to the rear. He launched into an angry explanation of the fight at the tavern, concluding, "The wizard struck a sore wound into one of my best men."

"Will the man live?" asked one of those at whom Magus stared.

A murmured conference, out of sight behind Magus. Then: "It appears so."

"Then the incident will be overlooked. Retire now."

More grumbling. A squeaking swing of a massive door. A bolt shooting home.

Silence.

Magus studied the half dozen men seated in front of him on the other side of a scarred but highly polished refectory table. The men wore monks' robes, denoting membership in the planet's bureaucracy. In addition each of the six wore a bright satin-lined hood pushed down behind the back of the neck. The hoods were of six different colors: a wintry blue, a bird's-wing orange, a flower yellow, a countryside green, a twilight purple, and, around the neck of the man who had spoken in a voice very much resembling a death rattle, a hood of sunrise scarlet.

The six were not imposing physically. One was very fat, another emaciated. The rest could hardly be distinguished from rabble, so common were their features. Not a one could be younger than seventy.

The one in the scarlet hood seemed to be in charge. He occupied the seat at the extreme end of the table on Magus' left. He had a pleasant face, with mild blue eyes and a thin mat of white hair across a shiny scalp.

Yet there was power in this stone-walled room that smelled of the damp underground and blazed with fifty burnished lamps in niches. Magus saw the power in the obvious distinction of the hoods, bright as the plumage of male birds. And Magus realized something else.

Such ordinary mortals could not be identified as High Governors unless each truly possessed that lofty station. They were too common for it to be otherwise.

The High Governor in the scarlet hood sniffed at Magus' aroma of ale, then began to speak.

"We have not provided you with a chair, wizard Magus Blacklaw, since we shall be brief. We have convened tonight from our respective areas of authority on Pastora as a result of the word we received earlier today about your appearance before the Cathedral Tribune. We have come here secretly in our skysleds because, out of hundreds of charlatans who from time to time pose as wizards on this planet, you stand forth."

A clammy itching on Magus' spine. He began to understand why the Cathedral Tribune had turned against the prosecutor. He didn't like this. Not at all. He said, "The High Governors flatter me."

"We are not here to flatter you," said the emaciated one, a tottering wreck of ninety or so. "We are here to charge you with a task."

"Task?"

"Behind us," spoke the Governor of the scarlet hood, "you will notice a tapestry."

Magus hadn't really seen it before. Now he looked closely. The tapestry covered almost all the wall, a strange, wild thing of golden whorls, coruscating green disks and smaller, pearly spheres in a random pattern, intricately stitched into the darkest of purple backgrounds.

"What we tell you now, wizard," said the obese Governor, "is privileged. There is only one punishment if you ever speak a syllable of what you are about to hear."

Magus fingered his collar. "You needn't elaborate. I understand." *Ah, Magus, my crow, my victim, something far worse than being arrested as a false wizard is brewing in this lamp-mad room. . . .*

"The tapestry," said the Governor of the scarlet hood, "is a map, or what purports to be a map, of the portion of the stars in which Pastora finds its place. Look carefully at left center. You can pick out this world, its sister Lightmark and our sun Graphos."

A nod showed them Magus had.

"The map is the ancient work of an ignorant man. But in a sense we are all equally ignorant. We suspect there were mighty cities on other worlds before the nuclear rains. We suspect that the pieces of magical apparatus you employed today may have been created rationally rather than demonically.''

"Yet since the rains," said another Governor, ''there has been doubt. Much doubt.''

In a sudden flash of insight, Magus felt sorry for these men. The most powerful humans on Pastora, they still could not help revealing their lack of knowledge and their naked fear.

Scarlet Hood commenced again: "It is not easy to seek light in an age of darkness. It is not easy to govern less fortunate men who cannot even read the few remaining book-rolls. To forestall chaos we govern by fear. We employ the very superstitions we sometimes doubt. Yet sometimes too, our blood, our heritage compels even us to believe those same superstitions and be cowed by them. Can you understand this much?''

Magus gave a nod, thinking, *Yes, I'm a man like you. Pastora's child. I shook when I held the chromium sphere in my hands*.

"Plainly put, Magus Blacklaw, our problem is this: the wealth of Pastora runs thin. Our resources dwindle. We cannot exist for many more generations before ruinous civil wars begin, and famines. And mass death. To prevent this, we believe we must break away from this world, find new wealth or rediscover old. In truth, we do this for the single purpose of maintaining the government which we represent. The government is all that stands between Pastora and a night of ruin. Even some of the old magical devices are failing. So we must find others. New sources of power and wealth against the day coming all too soon when our mines play out and our fields turn sour and rotten.''

"And there is a place," the fat governor put it, "where such magical devices are said to exist. A place within reach—"

Deep in Magus' mind, something cold sang the words before the first Governor pronounced them:

"The planet Lightmark."

Magus saw the trap closing. He did not see how he could escape. He managed to keep his voice calm as he answered: "So I have heard in occult communion with the spirits."

A little glimmer of amusement showed in the mild eyes of Scarlet Hood. Did they know? Did they recognize his sham? Were they merely playing with him to gain their own ends? No, he decided, not wholly.

The Governor in the scarlet hood said, "Once a great corporate house possessing many magical secrets flourished on Lightmark. It bore a name corrupted from a commercial name billions of years old, a name dating to the time of the Out-riding from the First Home. On Lightmark, it is told, the remains of this mighty house of Easkod still stand today. But its secrets are guarded by demons which only a true wizard can exorcise. We cannot go and do what must be done—perform the exorcism. We are too old. And we do not possess the magical skills. You have proved yourself master of such skills. You, Magus Blacklaw, in a skysled provided by the High Governors of Pastora, shall voyage to Lightmark and exorcise the demons, so that the way may be opened for exploration." The Governor paused, his mild eyes fixing hard on Magus as he finished, "If you are a true wizard, you will not be afraid."

The trap was closed.

Deny their command—admit he was a false wizard—and he was dead.

But how would he fare on Lightmark?

What about this talk of demons and demon-lairs? Was it all an uncertain pious fraud?

Hans Huygens had seen Brother Plume. He had been to Hauntplace.

Somehow, though, Magus found courage to smile at them.

"I accept the charge. I will go to Lightmark. I will perform the exorcism."

"It is agreed," said the High Governor in the scarlet hood. For one awful instant, Magus saw tears in the mild eyes.

The old men believed that the demons could be exorcised because they still believed the demons existed, despite everything reason told them.

A veined hand lifted in a fluttering wave of dismissal. "You will be informed concerning the time of your departure, wizard Magus Blacklaw. It will be made a day of celebration, planetwide. Go now and prepare."

Blindfolded, Magus was led out, and never saw the High Governors again.

IX

FOUR WAITED where he had expected one. Three carried swords.

It was twilight. A week had passed since his encounter with the High Governors. A lurid green sky hung over New Brussels. Moment by moment fat black clouds blotted out more and more of the light, driven ahead of a wind that smelled of rain.

Dressed in a fusty cloak with the cowl pulled up full over his head, Magus had slipped out of the inn by the back way. Whenever he went about the city uncowled now, a crowd of the curious soon gathered. They ran along after him, whining for supernatural favors or merely the touch of his hand. Thus he found himself almost anticipating the departure for Lightmark. At least in space he wouldn't be a public curiosity.

The greenish light had shrunk to a band running around the western horizon by the time he reached the quarter of the city he wanted. A few drops of rain pelted his face. Reddish lightning smeared the northwest. In this district most of the buildings were ramshackle produce sheds, shut down for the night. At the end of the lane to which Maya's hand-drawn map had guided him a high stone wall blocked further passage.

Behind the wall loomed a strange structure with many chimneys spouting drifts of whitish smoke. A rickety signboard attached to the wall clattered in the wind.

NEW BRUSSELS STEAMHOUSE, ENTRANCE BY OFFICIAL PERMIT ONLY.

The equipment inside the forbidden steamhouse had to do with keeping the city warm during the short winter. But beyond that, city steamhouses, like sky-sleds, fell into the domain of magic. The steamhouse operators were employees of the bureaucracy. They probably knew nothing about machinery save for which levers or handles or switches made it operate.

The four men waited under the outer wall, partially hidden behind a market cart that held half a dozen rotting cabbages. In the rainy green light Magus recognized the look of three of them—tall, thin men in garish yellow boots.

Hired bravos.

A dagger flashed as one of the bravos saw Magus approaching. The man tossing and catching the knife had a white scar on his chin. Magus stopped. He eased back his cloak so that he could get at his sword. He advanced no further.

A fourth man stepped from behind the abandoned cart. At a distance, his long graying hair and short, nearly white beard lent him an air of respectability his three companions lacked. The man's belly showed the effects of too much fattening food, or age, or both. It protruded under his threadbare brown doublet, contrasting with his extremely thin legs. The man walked in front of the bravos and raised his right gauntlet.

''Wizard? I'm the one who passed your daughter the

message in the perfume market. Please come down here. You have nothing to fear."

Magus hauled out his blade, a slithering sound.

"And I have nothing but your word to assure me of that."

But he moved ahead cautiously, reached the cart and halted again.

The bravos were typically thick-witted specimens, the kind in almost any city on the planet. Except for the scar-chinned one, they did not seem hostile. Rather, they displayed a certain curious interest in Magus' face and clothes. Still, it was best to be wary. Men like these would kill on order for a ha'credit.

Magus looked at the smaller man. "My daughter said you wanted to see me. That it would be to my advantage. She had your name scrawled on a scrap but I've lost it."

"Lantzman," the other answered. "Philosopher Arko Lantzman." Said with a weary pride.

Two things struck Magus forcibly: This Lantzman was not as old as his bulging belly and graying hair first suggested. He was no more than Magus' own age. But he showed the ravages of bad living. His clothes were patched in many places. His shoulders slumped. A cerebral man, Magus thought. Like old Phlebos, but without Phlebos' toughness and adaptability to the rigors of living catch-as-catch-can.

The second thing which struck him was Lantzman's haunted look. Above a wine-reddened nose, brown eyes moved ceaselessly.

"I don't know what the title Philosopher signifies," Magus told him.

"It's hereditary. The equivalent of a triple doctorate

in the old days when there were universitites to teach knowledge instead of governments to teach the fear of it.''

"You find it necessary to meet in a place like this? With bodyguards?"

"Yes," said Lantzman, with bitterness. "I am one of the heirs to something which the people of Pastora hate with the kind of hatred only ignorance can create. These bodyguards are paid for by a small inheritance left me when my wife's grandfather died. I find it a wise investment. Otherwise I live frugally."

Magus scowled. "I'm not interested in your financial habits or your geneology. You proposed a meeting in secret, saying it would be to my advantage. I assume you meant in terms of credits. If not, tell me and I'll leave."

The bravo with the chin scar snickered. He tossed his dagger up and caught it. The blade flashed with the last green light of the sky. It was raining harder. Magus pulled up his cowl.

"Forgive me. I'll make my point. Within the week you will depart for Lightmark under the auspices of the High Governors. Your charge is to exorcise the demons of the planet and rediscover, on behalf of the government, any existing ruins of the great commercial house that once flourished there."

"So far," Magus said, "you've only proved that you listen to public gossip."

Arko Lantzman bristled. "I can do more than that, wizard. I can tell you something about what you'll find on Lightmark."

Magus sucked in a breath. "You've been there?"

A shake of Lantzman's grayed head. "My wife's

grandfather died in exile here on Pastora years ago. Before that he was Chief Philosopher of Lightmark's great commercial house. The rabble would translate his title to mean chief wizard. Again you see the result of ignorance. He was correctly known as the scientific director of the corporation.''

"Of the House of Easkod?"

"Aye. It was the greatest firm of its kind before the nuclear rains. It specialized in the technology of image formation. Permanent records of the look of things. People. Places. Immutably registered and fixed by the apparatus which the corporation manufactured. They were the communicators. The carriers of knowledge throughout all of a galaxy in which this puny, pitiful little planet is but a mote. Theirs was the universal tongue. Without words. Their equipment produced what you naïvely called a picture of souls. That equipment, by the way, had to come from Lightmark. Where did you get it?''

"I don't like your tone, Philosopher. I told the Tribune I wouldn't answer that question."

Lantzman shrugged. "You also convinced the Governors that you are a wizard. Let us at least be honest with each other, Magus Blacklaw. There are no wizards. There is no magic. There are only natural principles which have been encrusted with layer after layer of superstition and misunderstanding.''

Exactly as old Phlebos said!

But Magus kept his face free of the surprise of it. He didn't care for this pudding-faced little man with the fanatic brown eyes.

"On Lightmark," Lantzman continued, "you will find the towers of Easkod still standing. They built well in the old days. The nuclear effects died long ago.

There should be no personal danger in entering the premises. But the scientific equipment you will find will be useless to you or anyone else without the proper key."

His hands fumbled at the bosom of his doublet. Rain trickled down his cheeks as he brought forth a small cube of gray metal that hung on a thin chain around his neck.

"Without this you'll be powerless, never be able to unlock all the riches that wait in Easkod."

Magus eyed the cube skeptically. "What riches?"

"The machines! The research devices! All in perfect working order! Capable of producing again! Of opening communications between the planets! Banishing fear! Restoring life to the way it was before the wars!"

"And that tiny thing is all I need?"

"Yes."

The rain grew harder. Magus shivered. Eyes shining, Lantzman went on:

"This cube can be likened to a philosopher's stone. Inserted in the proper aperture in the proper piece of equipment in the house of Easkod, it will make a million dead tongues speak. All the stored information —the accumulated wisdom of a hundred generations —will be available for perusal. With this cube lights will burn. Dynamos will roar. Think-machines will think. All the secrets of the great house will be secrets no longer."

"Why tell me?" Magus asked.

Lantzman's mouth wrenched. "False wizard or no, I need you. Just as you need this"—pudgy fingers handled the cube stroking it, caressing it—"which was handed down from my wife's grandfather to my wife.

This little cube kept me alive these past ten years since her death. I knew that regardless of how many indignities the rabble heaped on me—how many times I forced myself to remain silent when peasants prated about demons—it would be worth it. Staying alive for the sake of this cube has been my single goal. So I buy bodyguards . . .''

Was Lantzman crying or was it only rain streaming on his cheeks?

"When I reach Lightmark this will bring me power. Not power I want personally. Be clear on that. But I promised my wife as she promised her grandfather that the house would come to life. And so it will. We'll throw off this cursed darkness we wallow in and the lights will shine from Easkod again.''

Shaking a little, Lantzman licked his upper lip. He didn't see two of his bodyguards exchange sneers, as if to say, *A lunatic. But he buys our weapons. Why argue?*

"I still don't understand why—" Magus began.

"My problem," said Philosopher Arko Lantzman softly, "is simply to reach Lightmark.''

"If that cube is so magical—"

"Don't use that word! There is no magic! There are only the lost technologies people fear!''

For the moment Magus kept his counsel about Brother Plume and his band of holy wild men who guarded the corporation's abandoned towers. He said: "If that cube has such power, why not approach the High Governors?''

"Because I am a member of the family of a manager of a corporation! Easkod! As such I'm not even supposed to exist! I conceal my identity lest they execute me. I've lived on the run most of my life because people hate the memory of the commercial houses, and they blame them for the wars.''

"True. But I do know the Governors are interested in Lightmark now, for reasons of economics and otherwise. Surely you could approach—"

"They'd have my head in half an hour."

"Why so?"

"Because I'd laugh in their faces when they prate of demons. I'd call them monsters for hoarding the few scientific devices on Pastora to serve their own corrupted authority. There's no hope for me in the established channels. I know there are no demons on Lightmark—"

What of the Hauntplace? But again Magus said nothing.

"—and perhaps you know likewise, eh? But you're the one who gets passage to the sister planet on a government skysled. For me to try to steal one would be highly dangerous. It's much safer to approach you, don't you see? Strike a bargain. Half the wealth of Easkod.'' Lantzman seized Magus' forearm. He had the sick smell of desperation on him. "Half, that's what I'm offering you! Smuggle me aboard the skysled before it leaves! It should be no trouble. You'll be making the journey alone—"

"Wrong, Philosopher. My daughter and a young man are going with me." *At their insistence*, Magus thought bitterly. *And with my foolhardy assent.*

Lantzman blinked into the rain. "No matter. The details can be worked out."

"Exactly what wealth would we share? Suppose you start up all the pieces of scientific apparatus? What will they do? Manufacture ingots of precious metal? Spew out gems? You said yourself, Easkod's products were picture-making equipment.''

"The think-machines contain much other information. Valuable information!''

"Unless it's spendable, my friend, no thank you.''

As it stands now, I'm quite content to undertake the risks of the trip on the chance of finding and looting enough scientific apparatus to make my fortune at long last. And of course there's the additional reward of saving my own skin. Why ask for more trouble?

The green light had vanished from the sky. Window-lamps burned all over the city now. Magus was soaked and chilled. Philosopher Arko Lantzman closed his hand like a claw around the chained cube, protecting it. His lips were white.

"It will do you no good to report me to the High Governors. I'll be hiding as I've hidden before. I have made my offer. Well?''

"I am not interested.''

The bravos stirred. One slid forward, hefting his dagger. Magus took a step back. He fanned his cloak-edge away in case he had to haul out his sword. But Lantzman lifted a dark gauntlet.

"Let him go.'' He glared at Magus. "I only warn you of this. You've chosen not to come to terms with me. But I am not the only survivor of the House of Easkod. Before you're through you may find yourself forced to cooperate with persons less genteel and reasonable than I. Men who would reach Lightmark to rape the corporation, steal its secrets for their own personal gain.''

"You already offered me half,'' Magus reminded him.

"And with the other, goddamn you, I'd bring light and learning back to the whole galaxy!"

Slowly Magus shook his head. "I can't believe you."

"I'll not stay and argue with a sod like you. Good evening—*wizard*."

Tossing his cloak over his shoulder, Philosopher Arko Lantzman stumped away up the street past the produce sheds with his yellow-booted bravos trailing behind. The scar-chinned one threw Magus a last glance, as if to say it would be a pleasure to encounter him under the right circumstances. The bravo gave his dagger a flip, caught it and disappeared around a rain-swept corner.

Magus left the steamhouse and started back toward the inn, bundled deep in his cloak. He tried to laugh at the memory of Lantzman. But somehow that laughter sounded hollow in the wet, deserted streets.

Who were the others Lantzman had said he might encounter?

And how dangerous might they prove to be?

X

BELLS PEALED. Children threw flower petals. Thousands of doves whirled and swooped across the sunlit plain where the skysled lay in its cradle, needle prow angled up toward a sky full of racing clouds.

Nearly half a million citizens of New Brussels had swarmed to the plain at the city's edge before first light. They were kept away from the sleek gray-blue craft by authorities who had linked their arms to form a great circle around the launch cradle.

From inside the control canopy, Magus Blacklaw looked out the port at that human ocean of faces reaching all the way to the horizon where the bell towers of the city rose. Magus was strapped into a padded launch chair. To his right Maya lay similarly bound. Beyond her, to starboard, Robin drummed his fingers on the arms of his own chair and watched from the port on his side.

Across the curving console before them little colored lights flickered, racing faster now in the sequences preceding launch. An illuminated dial in the console's center swept off the moments with its large red hand. In less than two minutes the skysled would lift.

During their first hour on board Magus examined the walls of gauges, dials, indicators to the rear. He studied the think-machines. Inside the glass fronts of their metal cases silver memory drums revolved at blurring speed. Magus reluctantly concluded that he didn't have the knowledge necessary to work the mechanisms and take control of the flight once it had begun.

The skysled was programmed for a direct course to Lightmark. Magus had been given a book-roll which listed the steps he must take to restart the skysled for its return journey. But this process could be set in motion only after the skysled touched down on the sister planet.

Maya sensed his uneasiness. She wriggled her hand in the wrist-strap until she could touch his fingers.

"We'll come through this, Father. We've endured worse times."

"But I just don't know what I'm doing! If there are demons to be exorcised, damned if I know how to go about it."

Robin's gold eyes caught sunlight as he turned his head. "I've still got my sword."

"We'll probably need it."

The scarlet sweep hand reached the last minute. Magus grew angry with himself. *Damned if I'll yap and whine any more. We'll take Lightmark, just the three of us. We'll pull its forked tail and make it yelp.* . . .

Robin Dragonard's hand stretched over to close around Maya's. Her violet eyes were warm as she looked at the young man. The scarlet hand stood straight up on the illuminated dial.

A subdued but steady roaring began behind them.

The skysled vibrated. Magus saw the monk-robed bureaucrats genuflecting down on the plain. *Spiritual blessings? How useful!*

His neck chafed. Around it he wore a gridded, wafer-like device on a thin elastic band. The device had been supplied to him for reporting his progress back to Pastora. A turn of a tiny switch on the wafer's surface supposedly activated the unit. How the little apparatus could cast his voice the long distance between planets he didn't know. More magic!

Suddenly Maya's fingers bit his arm. Terror shone on her face. There was a sound like a great crack. The skysled thundered off the cradle, spaceborne.

In seconds they were tearing up through the clouds. The skysled rattled and vibrated. The memory drums on the guidance think-machines whirred so fast they became invisible.

The sky darkened. The clouds plummeted away below. Out of the port Magus saw reflections on the guidance vanes of the fire streaming from their tail.

The skysled broke out of the atmosphere into the arching black of space. Graphos burned gaseously purple above them. The little firelights of a host of suns spangled the limitless distances with orange and deep red and blue-white. Maya wept at the beauty.

Somewhat less demonstrative, the two men unstrapped themselves from the launch chairs and ran to fetch the wineskins they'd smuggled aboard.

An hour later, Magus and Robin were drunk and feeling jolly. With a crazily cocked eyebrow Magus regarded the view out past the needle prow.

A week to reach Lightmark? Well, a man could bear

all this light-spangled lonesomeness if he were sodded enough. To come upon it unprepared—he wouldn't care for that.

"Did you ever see anything so gorgeous?" Maya asked no one in particular.

Robin burped. "Makes me feel like a flea on the belly of one of my sheep."

"My sentiments exactly," Magus said. "Pass me another drink, boy."

"You shouldn't order Robin around that way, Father." Maya was only half teasing.

"Be damned! Isn't he going to be my son-in-law? I'm just getting him trained."

Maya flushed. Robin laughed. Magus watched the stars-and-black ahead and tried not to tremble.

Maya burst into the control canopy. Ashen, she hung on the edges of the hatchway.

"Robin's found him, Father. They're fighting—"

Instantly Magus unfolded himself from the launch chair. His hand whipped toward the blade at his wrist, slid it free as he dodged sideways past the girl and began to run down the metal corridor between the glowing think-machines.

It was the third morning of an untroubled flight. Magus had learned to move with some speed in the sled's artificial gravity. Ahead, past the large chamber where an open catwalk ran above humming modules, Magus saw the storage hold. Between lashed-down crates of rations Robin Dragonard was struggling with a cloaked man. And getting the worst of it.

So Maya wasn't hallucinating! Magus thought as he hit the power chamber and raced on across the catwalk.

Twice in the past two days his daughter had reported

seeing someone hiding in the dim storage hold. An indistinct figure. No more than a suggestion of a man. Each time a thorough search netted no results. Magus marked it down to overactive imagination, an emotional reaction brought on by the silent immensity of space. After acceleration the skysled's power modules had damped themselves. The craft was arrowing through airlessness without noise.

That Robin had discovered a flesh-and-blood stowaway was all too evident. Muffled in cloak and cowl, the man smashed Robin under the chin.

Robin crashed against a teetering stack of crates. The stowaway leaped forward to kick his head. Robin rolled out of the way. Magus jumped into the storage hold, ready with his sword. The stowaway's boot missed as Robin rolled again and scrambled up with murder in his gold eyes.

The stowaway heard Magus coming. From under his dun cloak he whipped a hand weapon with a long rod-like muzzle. Magus laughed. The stowaway danced aside. Magus' blade tore the side of a crate. A ripped plastic storage bladder inside it rained nutrient pills onto the metal floor.

Cursing, Magus hauled his blade free and crouched around. The stowaway backed off, index finger wrapped around the hand weapon's trigger-stub. Robin hunched in beside Magus. Their shoulders touched. Pair of blades glittering, they started at the stranger.

"This is a very old weapon but still an efficient one," said the cowled man in a voice Magus thought he should remember. "It can burn your heads off before you take another three steps. It might cripple the sled as well. I certainly don't want that. I doubt you do either."

Maya slipped into the hold, watching her father hesitate.

Suddenly Magus knew the voice.

He lowered his sword and stalked forward. With his free hand he shoved the cowl aside.

A long, tough face. Calculating eyes. Shaggy red eyebrows and moustache—

"You were in the hall at my second trial."

"Aye, and I asked you about Lightmark."

"You've been stowed away since before the launch?"

"Correct again. It took some doing. I left one authority with a new mouth in his neck the night before the sled took off. I buried him in a drainage ditch, stole his uniform and got aboard. Once or twice this pretty young lady interrupted me when I came out of hiding looking for something to eat."

The stranger walked to a stack of crates in that long, loping stride Magus had noticed before. The man banged a scarred fist on the crates. A hollow sound came back.

"Before you boarded I emptied these crates and cut an opening into the other side, against the bulkhead. I knew I'd have to come out eventually. I'm damned hungry."

There was a certain politeness about the stranger. He was not an uneducated man, Magus decided. Yet his eyes were oddly cold, failing to echo any little smile that showed on his mouth.

"I have a meal in mind for you," Robin grumbled, hefting his sword.

The stranger spoke to Magus in a low, steady voice. "Tell the boy to hold his peace or I'll use the blaster on him. I intend to reach Lightmark on this sled with or without all of you. Be civil and there's no need for killing.''

Magus nodded to Robin. "Put your sword up."

Robin's gold eyes glared. But after a moment he obeyed.

Maya watched the stranger with a certain rapt fascination as he shoved the weapon into his wide belt and said:

"There have been no hand blasters manufactured since before the wars. Mine was passed down to me by my father. As I said, very old, but it works. Let it be a constant reminder. Now, I made a polite request about something to fill my stomach. I know you've a galley. I almost got there twice. Perhaps this is the time . . .''

The stranger took a step toward the power chamber. Magus blocked his way.

"Questions first."

A bushy red eyebrow hooked up. "And if I don't answer will you stop me with magic?"

Magus went scarlet, raising his sword. Abruptly the stranger laughed.

"In the Tribune hall, wizard, I knew you were a clever man even if you are a trickster. Now I can tell you're a man of guts too. Very well. Questions. I know the first one. My name is William Catto. I am the grandson of the last Prime Manager of the Easkod Corporation of Lightmark. In case you're not familiar with the term, Prime Manager was the title given the highest operating officer of a commercial house. Like so many others, my grandfather was forced into exile on Pastora after the nuclear rains. I've been seeking a way to Lightmark for a good long time."

Magus had the eerie feeling he'd heard it before. The wasted face of Philosopher Arko Lantzman swam in memory. Was this fierce, red-moustached man one of the others to whom Lantzman had made reference?

"What do you want on Lightmark?" Magus asked.

William Catto shrugged. He smiled lazily at Maya. She looked quickly away.

"I want the resources of Easkod. They're rightfully mine. Do you know anything about the corporation? You had some of its equipment with you in the Tribune hall. . . ."

"To answer the question you put to me then, I've never been on Lightmark."

"I imagined as much from the amateurish way you operated the apparatus. Well, before the wars Easkod specialized in the technologies of visual communication. These sprang from a very ancient science that's said to have originated on the First Home. *Photographos.* Light-writing, in the old tongue. Your picture of souls as you called it—an unfinished negative image—was formed by an adaptation of the light-writing process. All this is part of the heritage my grandfather the Prime Manager lost when the corporations closed down on the eve of the nuclear wars. He was forced into hiding. Damned as a war-maker. Learning has been scorned since that time, but now it seems to be emerging from under the cloud. At least if I read the interest of the High Governors aright. I intend to arrive at Lightmark first, find Easkod and rebuild the corporation."

Magus was struck speechless by the quiet audacity of Catto's statement. Rebuild a great house single-handed? A madman's dream surely. Then Magus noted Catto's intense, somber stare. Perhaps the man was determined enough—or mad enough—to do it.

Catto took Magus' silence for deep interest. "One

day soon, you know, all the great companies will function again. Their knowledge isn't gone, only buried. It will be precious when the time comes to reopen the II Galaxy to normal trade. The men who take control of the corporations now will be powerful men when that happens. I intend to be the one controlling Easkod.''

Magus let out a breath. ''There are demons on Lightmark, Catto.''

''So we're told. I don't know one way or the other. I'll worry when I meet them.''

''I've been sent to exorcise them.''

''Yes. Of course.'' Catto nodded sardonically. ''If you can.''

Magus scowled. He both disliked and respected the man's nerve. And was more than a little wary of his quiet fanaticism.

Magus thought it over while Robin glared. Maya never took her eyes from the stranger. At length Magus said:

''The skysled is programmed. We can't turn it back. And that weapon you carry, if it works—''

''It does.'' Catto said it flatly, in the manner of a warning.

''—may be of help to us. Therefore we'll make a truce. Take him to the galley, Maya.''

Catto smiled. ''A wise choice. Even if it was your only one.''

As Maya led William Catto from the storage hold, Magus wondered whether he'd regret his decision. Robin Dragonard let out a curse of rage and clattered his sword back into its scabbard.

Magus put his hand on Robin's shoulder to reassure him; Robin pulled away and stalked off without looking back.

Four days out.

Graphos was long gone behind them. Gigantic orange suns pinwheeled above and below, throwing out long gaseous arms that blazed against the dark space. The skysled flew silently except for the faint hum of the mysterious machines which kept it on course and maintained its artificial gravity and atmosphere.

Freshly wakened from sleep, Magus walked into the control section.

A wash of orange light filtered through the upper control canopy, flooding William Catto's red hair, making it glow. Catto lounged in the right-hand launch chair. Maya sat in the left-hand one. Fingers locked beneath her chin, she stared at Catto as he spoke.

"—so I've probably tramped every road on Pastora. It's wise to keep moving and keep silent too. Survivors of the great houses can't stay in one place or brag about their ancestors if they care to survive."

"Have you ever been to the Southern Ice?" Maya asked.

"Once, for a twelve-month. I hunted the little white fur-fangs. When I sold the pelts I made enough credits to live for another six-month."

"Most people avoid the Ice. Even when times were lean, my father never wanted to go there."

Catto noticed Magus. Maya hadn't yet. Catto smiled. "Certainly it couldn't have been from a lack of courage. Your father is plainly a brave man."

"Thank you," Magus said. "I also have thin blood, dislike the discomforts of low temperatures and refuse to perform for a pack of stinking hunters who can only pay in hides. Maya, it's time for a little evening food. Where's Robin?"

"Probably sulking," Maya said with a toss of her

russet hair. "This trip seems to be bringing out a vile streak in his temper. I'll come to the galley as soon as William finishes telling me about the Southern Ice. He—"

"I heard." Magus turned and went out.

Incredible, how his daughter hung upon Catto's every word. He hoped Maya's interest was only temporary. Magus regarded William Catto as a dangerous man.

A plague on being a father, he thought as he stormed back to the galley for a drink.

Five days out.

The skysled was ghosting through a cluster of milky suns. The black space faded behind the luminescence that swept around them and gleamed from the skysled's vanes.

Magus reckoned their days aboard the sled by a realtime device on the main control console. The device told him it was time for another routine inspection.

Not that he comprehended the workings of the sled's machinery. But some of the devices, notably the power modules in the chamber under the catwalk, were marked. The power-damping rods carried little painted inscriptions which said that in the damped attitude the rods must not project past red indicator lines. Every evening Magus climbed down the ladder from the catwalk and inspected each module with its bristle of a dozen rods. He did so now, satisfying himself that no rod projected past the line painted upon it. Satisfied that everything was in good order tonight, he seized the ladder handrails, starting up. He noticed Robin on the catwalk.

"Hallo, Robin! I haven't seen you since morning."

Robin leaned on the catwalk rail. He hadn't used depilatory. His gold eyes were hooded, sullen. "I wasn't aware that anybody aboard was particularly interested in my welfare."

Hauling himself up the ladder, Magus laughed. "Spoken like a jealous tomcat."

Robin seized his arm. "Don't talk to me that way! You may be her father, but you're not mine."

Magus sucked a breath between his teeth. "Take your hands off me, Robin, or I'll teach you a few courtesies. Painfully."

With a sharp sigh Robin let go. "Why in hell I ever shipped on with you—"

"You asked to come. I advised against it." He laid a hand on Robin's shoulder. This time the younger man didn't pull away. "Look, lad. I dislike Catto as much as you do. I'm sure he'd burn me with that hand blaster if I tried to balk him. But he speaks well and he's traveled widely on Pastora. Where's the harm if Maya listens to him? She's a bright girl. She'll sense his hardness soon enough."

Robin gnawed his lip, unconvinced. "If he puts his scummy hands on her . . ."

"I don't believe he will. But if it happens, be careful. He's killed before. Look in his eyes. You can see it."

Swearing under his breath, Robin left. Magus was only mildly amused. Jealous rage wasn't desirable in these cramped surroundings.

Well, in two more days they'd reach Lightmark. Earlier Magus might have considered this a curse. Now it began to look more like a blessing.

In his yeasty dreams that night, Serafina, the widow of New Delft, pulled silver pins from her hair and let it tumble red and inviting down across her bare, milky shoulders, down across her bare—

Suddenly Serafina's mouth went O-shaped. She cried out.

The piercing sound tumbled Magus away from her, sent him spinning over and over in dream-fall—

Cold and tense, he wakened in the metal-smelling dark of his cramped bunk. The howl in his ears was the howl of a klaxon.

He lunged from bed, pulled on his tunic and kicked open the hatch of the tiny sleeping cubicle. Just as he stepped into the hall, a figure bowled past him. All at once Magus heard a faint voice crying for help.

"Maya!"

He plunged after the running man in the night-lit corridor. The man ahead was faster, turning left down a short L-walk, then right again into the main companionway. Magus recognized Catto by the blaze of his red hair.

Catto reached the power chamber. He jumped from the catwalk to the floor below. A blinding-white brilliance sheened the air, hurting Magus's eyes as he staggered onto the catwalk.

Instantly he saw a girl's slipper caught in an open seam of the catwalk. Beside it lay a tiny servotray and flask in which nutrient fluid sloshed back and forth. The flask was starred, as though it had fallen hard.

The white light poured from a single rod hole in one of the power modules. The light generated heat Magus could feel in his blood. He staggered to the rail, trying to see what was happening below.

Dimly he made out a slumped figure. A moment later he recognized his daughter. She must have been returning from the galley, caught her slipper in the imperfect seam, fallen—

And one of the damping rods had come out of the power module. All the way out past the telltale red mark. The murderous high-energy light blazed from the tiny opening, making his retinas burn.

He stumbled toward the ladder leading downward.

"Stay there, Blacklaw!" Catto bawled from somewhere in the white flare. "I'll hand her up to you."

Spears of white light dug deeper and deeper into his head, throbbing, hurting. He stretched out his hands.

Naked except for a pair of sleeping drawers, William Catto heaved Maya up on his shoulder. He got both hands beneath her. He raised her like a slab of butchered meat. The whiteness filled every cranny of Magus' mind. He groped for her shoulder as Catto grunted, thrusting her higher.

Dizzy with the white light, Magus lost his balance. He started to pitch forward off the catwalk. His left hand speared out, seized the rail, closed, held on.

His lungs burned as he pulled himself upright again. He bent forward.

"All right," he shouted. "Hold her a little higher—a little—*got her!*"

One hand on her shoulder, one under her knees, Magus straightened. He fought for balance. Then he spun away from the glaring white light and lowered Maya to the catwalk. As he crouched over her, someone bumped against him.

He heard Robin's strangled voice: "Is she—?"

Maya's throat against his left ear gave off a faint *lub-lubba*. "Still breathing." He turned back to the rail. "Catto? Where are you?"

In the whiteness flooding against his eyes he saw a quick-moving shadow, hands grasping a sheared rod. From the depths of the glow Catto called:

"She must have snapped off one of the damp rods when she fell. I'll try to put it back—Ah, goddamn!"

A clatter. Catto dropped the rod.

Magus gripped the rail, stared downward. The heat in his blood was tangible pain now, as though everything inside him broiled. The whiteness from the hole in the power module grew whiter still, a whiteness that enveloped, choked, drowned—

Sudden dark.

Then the sound of William Catto's exhausted panting.

"—rammed the stub home," he said as he crawled up the ladder. "Hope it lasts us the rest of the trip."

Catto reeled onto the catwalk. His chest ran with sweat. He blinked rapidly.

"You all right?"

Magus nodded.

Catto sucked in huge draughts of air. He held the rail, head down, back bowed in pain.

"I . . . wasn't sleeping . . . heard her yell. . . . How is she?"

He slumped on one knee. He touched Maya's left eyelid, lifted it and let it fall back. Then he listened to her breathing.

"Think she'll be all right. I was on an illegal skysled once years ago. A module rod blew as we landed. We got out but I remember the pilot telling me that ten minutes was about the max for a human system. The energy backflow, I mean. The white light. I don't think she got enough for it to be lethal."

Strange winking lights still danced at the back of

Magus' eyeballs. He heard Robin say: "I suppose you want everybody on their knees thanking you."

"Damn you, Robin," Magus said, "this is no time to let your jealousy—"

"Why, yes," Catto interrupted. "I suppose I do expect some thanks. But I suppose that's expecting too much from a child with a snot-running nose and a mouth to match."

Robin Dragonard growled, kicked past Magus and fastened his hands on Catto's throat.

Catto drove his knee up under Robin's jaw, smashing him back against the catwalk rail. Robin flailed. Head hanging a little, fists doubled into weapons, Catto sidled forward. Killing glittered in his eyes. He was smiling.

Magus drove the dizziness out of his head, hurled himself between them.

"*No!* We've saved a life and we aren't going to lose another."

He looked hard into Robin's gold eyes. Then he glanced back to Catto. He didn't like what he saw in either place.

He shoved Robin's chest. "You go to the galley. Catto, you help me bring Maya up front."

Silence. Hesitation. Robin and Catto stared at one another. Magus tensed again.

William Catto shrugged. "Sure, all right. The girl is the important one."

Maya was breathing normally when they carried her forward. They saw for the first time a green-and-pearl ball that must be Lightmark, straight ahead and growing larger.

For Magus it was none too soon.

XI

Tensions and angers were almost forgotten when they first saw the spires of Easkod.

On the morning of the seventh day the skysled descended into Lightmark's thin but breathable atmosphere. The aft rockets spurted. The craft's guidance vanes began to glow a cherry color. The skysled shot into an orbit carrying it from the planet's dark side over the great light-splashed curvature of the day side, and back into dark again.

Magus and the others unstrapped from their launch chairs. From the height of the orbit it was impossible to see much detail on the wrinkled brown land mass that seemed to cover most of the planet. Here and there a few pale aquamarine patches flashed, small seas. Otherwise Lightmark looked barren, and hostile. Magus was reassured by an absence of bluish haze or halations. The aftereffects of the nuclear rains no longer threatened.

The skysled shot out of the dark side again. The aft rockets thundered, damped, thundered. Watching through the canopy, Maya squeezed her father's hand hard.

William Catto leaned against a port, his lips curled up in a cat's grin. The navigation devices angled the skysled downward. Soon immense brown crags separated by dry purplish watercourses floated beneath them.

The craft flew over foothills. Magus' throat grew dry. Ahead stretched a rock-studded plain, inhospitable and arid. The plain was broken by a few humped ridges where skimpy blue-leafed vegetation tossed in a brisk wind. The shadow of the skysled raced along the plain's floor.

On the side of the control room away from Catto, Robin watched the red-moustached man with unfriendly interest. Since the incident in the power chamber Robin had said little to anyone. Magus knew trouble was brewing, was uncertain about how to prevent it.

Maya had recovered with no ill-effects save a day's nausea and lethargy. She had thanked Catto too many times over. That made Robin even more sullen.

Luckily, Catto treated Robin's silent rage as he would a child's: worthy only of being ignored. At the moment, as the skysled swooped closer and closer toward the ground, Catto concentrated on the horizon ahead.

"We're almost down," Robin announced. "Hold onto the chair bar, Maya."

"I can take care of myself, thank you."

Robin colored. Suddenly Catto pointed, exclaiming:

"There! I'm sure I saw—*yes!*"

His expression was almost beatific. Magus squinted, caught sight of spire-shapes floating in the haze to the north. Abruptly the skysled's retros boomed. The craft bounced down on its belly-skids, raising a wake of dust and pumice.

Before the skysled stopped rocking, Catto rushed out of the chamber and undogged the main hatch. A whistling, as pressure equalized. Magus followed the red-moustached man into the open air of Lightmark.

Catto hung on the rail of the stairs that had unfolded to the ground. The air made Magus giddy for a moment. It was heavy, dusty, warm. Catto's teeth glared as he laughed and pointed again.

"The machines of the High Governors calculated well. There it is. Twenty leagues away at most."

Magus followed the pointing finger. On the northern edge of the plain, their bases obscured by what appeared to be blowing dust, rose the slim and starkly beautiful towers of Easkod. Unblemished, as Hans Huygens had said. They shone. Magus counted several dozen and lost track.

"I've never seen anything so tall," Maya whispered.

"Ten thousand times taller than man." Catto grinned. "Come on, let's unload the stores. We can be there in two or three days."

He started back up the stairs. Robin blocked the hatch. Catto halted near the top step.

"Get out of the way, boy. There's work to be done."

"Not on your orders," Robin answered.

"None of that!" Magus cried. "Stand aside."

With another hostile glance at Catto, Robin ducked back inside. Maya was oblivious, studying the slim towers thrusting up in the north haze like silvered hands.

They unshipped as many packs of stores as they

could carry comfortably. Then Magus went back aboard, announcing that he'd make a final inspection to determine whether they'd left anything important.

He walked swiftly to the control canopy. There he pried his fingers into a little cavity under the bottom edge of one of the launch chairs.

One by one he drew out the few articles he'd managed to smuggle aboard on Pastora. A colorful handful of silks. A few packets of greenish fireball powder. His red sash silver-stitched with the cabalistic markings. He'd found these bits of equipment useful in difficult spots before. They might be so again.

Shoving up his tunic, he buckled on the last item taken from his cache. It was a coarse-cloth belt with several small pockets. He cinched the final buckle against the flat muscle of his belly, stuffed the various items into the pockets, smoothed his tunic into place and left the chamber.

Outside, he dogged down the hatch. They started tramping north.

The morning sun grew hotter. The plain was roughly V-shaped, bounded on both sides by continuous ridges studded with the blue-leafed shrubs that tossed in the wind. The apex of the plain was lost in the haze near Easkod.

As Magus maintained the pace, he began to feel contemptuous of the rabble on the home world. That reminded him of something.

He snapped the dial-switch on the wafer at his throat. He announced that they had arrived safely, were proceeding toward the corporation. He further reported that he had already encountered several demons and exorcised them into nothingness. Both the nature of the demons and the methods used were deliberately left vague. Then he turned the switch off, hoping the High Governors had heard him across the distance.

Magus began to suspect that Hans Huygens might have been soft in the head. But it wouldn't do to encourage the Governors this soon. The thought of looting enough apparatus to make himself rich was tantalizing him again.

What if he could get back to Pastora in the skysled without detection, land in some isolated place like the Southern Ice? If he could pull it off, he'd be forever free of the burden of making his living from magical shows. Let William Catto remain among his deserted towers! Magus Blacklaw had other things in mind, including a certain widow of New Delft.

It was all a kind of glorious, sun-hazed dream, born of sudden confidence counteracting long despair. It persisted into the afternoon, as they marched on down the plain, pausing only to chew sticky blocks of nutrient and rest briefly in the scraggly shade of a blue bush.

Graphos set in the northeast. The towers on the horizon turned a ruddy scarlet, then fell into shadow as the stars came out. The twilight air drained the land of its heat. Magus suggested retiring to the ridge to pitch camp. No one objected. Catto was in good spirits, taking long strides and humming as he went.

Catto preceded them toward the ridge. He was halfway up the near slope when he stiffened.

He cocked his head, listening. Magus thought he heard a rattle of shale. Suddenly Catto scrambled down toward them, wig-wagging his arms.

"Something on the other side—can't quite tell what. Better take cover. Try those rocks until we see—"

Robin exhaled suddenly. In the drowning red light of evening his face wrenched as he stared at the ridgeline. Magus saw it a second later. His blood turned slow and sickly inside him.

He caught Maya around the waist, thrust her into cover of the clust of rocks where Catto already crouched. Shadow after spindly black shadow rose on the ridge, sunset-etched, nightmarish. Magus' lips were white as he whispered:

"Hans Huygens didn't lie to us. There *are* Brothers."

Catto twisted toward him. "Brothers?"

"Creatures who guard Easkod. Human once, perhaps. They speak our tongue. A freebooter who said he'd been on Lightmark told me of them."

Maya's knuckles went to her mouth. "Human? No more. *No more!*"

Ten tall and bony Brothers appeared in a silent mounted line on the ridge.

Their beasts were four-legged, deep-chested. Lizard hides shone moistly. Long forked tails switched back and forth. Oversized slabbish heads on spindly necks moved fluidly left and right, up and down. Dumb eyes rolled.

On each beast sat a Brother with a quiver of short spears hanging over one shoulder. Like their mounts, the Brothers were scale-hided. The sinking sun accentuated the redness of their armored flesh. Each rider wore his little kilt, as Huygens had described. Their eyes stood out from their scaly foreheads and turned far in the sockets, white balls with huge black centers.

"Maybe they won't see us," Robin murmured.

"They already have," Catto said.

One of the Brothers snatched a spear out of his

quiver. He whipsawed the spear back and forth in some sort of signal, urging his mount forward down the side of the ridge. The rest of the Brothers followed.

A drumming shook the earth as the ridgers converged on the tumble of rocks where Magus and the others hid. Across the plain drifted a high *scree-scree* from the throats of the creatures.

A spear clanged against the rock just over Magus' head. Another. Robin batted a third aside.

Magus drew his sword half out, thrust it back with a curse. He ducked down and seized the only useful weapon he could find—a sharp, melon-sized rock.

Making that ear-hurting *scree-scree*, the Brothers poured down around the rocks half to one side, half to the other. Magus flung the rock. Robin threw another. Maya took up two and let them fly.

A Brother thundering past on his hairy-footed beast caught one of the rocks on the bony ridge that bisected his eyes. He squealed, nearly toppled. A rider beside him pushed at him, kept him from falling. The pack thundered away.

Their charge past the rocks had left a dozen spears on the ground but no one injured. Magus knew their luck couldn't last.

He caught up two, three of the short spears as the Brothers thundered away down the plain, pulled up, swung around to re-form their line and charge again. Their hairless, scaly heads reflected the last shafts of daylight.

The creatures rode back at the rock, crying their thin *scree* cry. Legs planted wide, Magus transferred a single spear to his right hand. When the Brothers were almost on him, he threw hard.

A spear flashed past his head. Another hit the rock behind him, striking sparks. His own cast skittered off the side of one of the beasts. Robin threw. His spear gouged a wound in a creature's shoulder. There was a flash of ooze.

Dust rose around the rock. Raging, tight-bellied, Magus hurled another spear into the confusion of racing mounts and chittering riders. Another—

A pale-sizzling ring of whiteness leaped past his shoulder. It circled the head of the nearest rider. There was a smell of burning.

The Brother engulfed in white light let out a hideous cry, pitched from his mount. Kicking and butting, the riderless beast went off at an angle. It bowled into other riders, biting at them with maddened jaws.

A Brother shrieked, drove two spears defensively into the wild beast's neck. It plowed down into the shale, lashing its forked tail back and forth. The half-spears stuck up into the twilight as it died.

The Brothers thundered on, retreating far down the plain this time.

William Catto took a tighter grip on his hand blaster. "I didn't want to fire more than once. There aren't too many charges left, and I've only one extra cylinder."

Suddenly Maya uttered a low cry. "They're leaving. The weapon drove them off."

Magus saw it was true. The Brothers angled the heads of their mounts back up to the ridge. They slunk over it and melted into the darkness.

A last forked tail disappeared. A drumming of beast-feet died away. Magus drew a heavy breath. He walked to where Catto stood, watching the ridgeline and rubbing his moustache with one finger.

"The weapon did save us," Magus said. "We owe you thanks."

A tiny purplish moon had crept up over the opposite ridge. By its light Catto's black eyes shone unreadable.

"In spite of what you may think, Magus, I'm not without feelings. I wouldn't let three people die just because of foolish words." A pointed glance at Robin. "I hope we're finished with those things. They are humanform. Changed by the rains, maybe? In any case, let's hope they're gone." Catto thrust the hand blaster into his belt.

A sudden, piping cry of pain startled Magus. He spun, saw something crawling through the shale not far off.

"The one you downed, Catto. He's still alive."

"Let's look," Catto said.

The four of them ran from the rocks to the place where the fallen Brother lay writhing.

XII

THE CREATURE SPRAWLED under the high-sailing moon, the right half of its torso crisped away by Catto's blaster.

Magus thrust Maya around behind him. He wrinkled his nose.

Beneath the creature the shale glistened and stank.

The Brother sensed their presence. White balls of eyes glared. The immense black pupils expanded and contracted rapidly.

"Apparently they can die like the rest of us," Catto grunted. The coldness was back in his voice.

The Brother let out a feeble *scree*. The thing kicked the shale as though in pain, his right knee-joint articulating clumsily under the small overlapped plates of his hide. Where his kilt rode up Magus saw proof that the mutants reproduced much as man did.

"Desecrators," the Brother piped. The slit-like mouth snapped shut on each word. "Desecrators."

"And many more of us to come," Catto said.

"How many Brothers are you?" Magus asked.

"As the pieces of the land."

The Brother scrabbled his chitinous claw in the shale, let a dozen more flinty chips trickle out. There were thousands of similar chips on the plain. A chill crawled up Magus' spine as the Brother repeated: "As the pieces of the land. You have desecrated. You will be punished."

"By what authority do you defend this place?" Magus asked.

The white-ball eyes rolled. "Do not blaspheme. It has been so since time forgotten."

"Or at least since the nuclear rains poisoned the planet," Magus breathed.

Robin grunted agreement. The creature thrashed. More of the stinking ooze leaked from the wreck of his chest cavity. The skin plates of his face lent him a certain rigidity of expression. But there was no mistaking the hate in his dying, whistling voice.

"Brother Plume's vengeance will be mighty. Brother Plume will come with many. With many—"

Catto nudged Magus. An eyebrow hooked up, questioning.

"Plume's the leader, I've heard."

Catto nodded as the creature waved his clawhand at the stars.

"There will be as many Brothers as the lights of heaven. Plume will lead them. You will be sent to the Hauntplace to see the demons that burn the mind. In the Hauntplace . . . Plume will take his revenge . . . in the Hauntplace—*aiiigahhh!*"

The Brother's head snapped back. Fresh ooze glistened. Thin white membranes closed down over the distended eyes. The Brother was dead.

The wind keened off the ridges.

"At least we can cover him," Robin said. He began to pitch handfuls of shale over the corpse.

Catto wasn't interested in such niceties. He took Maya's elbow protectively, drew her away. Robin didn't fail to notice.

Presently Magus threw on a last handful of shale. He dusted his palms and jerked his head to Robin to indicate that they should start marching. Robin hardly comprehended. His eyes were molten, furious.

Leaving the rocks with as many spears as they could carry, they moved down the plain again.

Catto swung into step beside Magus. He asked about the Hauntplace.

"Another tale," Magus replied. "It's a place that may exist here on Lightmark. Or possibly it's the state of a man's own mind when the Brothers overcome him. I can't say. Whatever it is, let's hope the prophecy doesn't come true." He hurried to catch up with Maya.

His daughter's step was faltering. She rubbed the back of one wrist against eyes puffed with weariness. Magus helped her walk for the better part of an hour. Finally he called a halt.

They found a sizable cairn which afforded good cover. They chewed more of the sticky hunks of nutrient and settled down for the night. Magus took the first watch. He knew he couldn't sleep easily.

The attack of the Brothers had left him shaken. He watched the ridgelines, starting at small night noises. After a time he grew drowsy. He lay down gratefully when Robin took over.

Magus' dreams were strained. Phantom hordes of the snake-necked beasts plunged across stormy skies, each with a Brother astride, each Brother crying blood down the cloud-strewn wind of his nightmare.

Fatigued, Magus rose shortly after sunup. They

marched on through the morning without further incident. Conversation remained at a minimum. Maya walked with Catto. Magus kept his eye on Robin because he was afraid the young man neared the explosion point.

When Graphos stood directly above they paused for another meal. Once more Magus turned on the throat-wafer. He spoke for ten minutes to the invisible listeners on Pastora.

He reported glowing results in his campaign to rid Lightmark of demons, stating categorically that he had already exorcised and dispatched several score. The whole business struck him as pointless in the light of their current situation. However, the High Governors seemed more and more unreal and distant, superstitious old idiots unequipped to face or deal with the realities of Lightmark as they really existed. He knew he was only spinning the Governors yarns that would please them. He intended to perform all his exorcisms with sword and spear and Catto's hand blaster. But why try to explain that to them? Very likely they'd disbelieve him anyway.

As they moved on and the sun slanted into afternoon, Magus began to have the uneasy feeling that they were being watched.

Several times he turned sharply, thinking he saw a movement on the ridgeline to the right. Each time the ridge was empty, only the blue bushes dancing in the breeze. He said nothing to the others. He scored himself for having an overworked imagination. Yet the feeling persisted down to the hour they made night camp at another cairn.

Even Catto looked tired now. Magus volunteered for the first watch. None of the others protested. They rolled into their cloaks and soon breathed steadily in sleep.

Magus moved to the eastern side of the cairn. He sat down with his back against a boulder to watch.

The ridgeline lay empty against the starred sweep of the sky. Magus heard a noise. A rattle of shale, barely perceptible in the wind. His neck crawled.

He kept his head bent low as though dozing. At the same time he slid his right hand across and pulled his sword, keeping it close to his thigh so it wouldn't glitter. The noise behind the ridge repeated, as though men crawled there. He heard a cough, quickly stifled.

Magus jumped up. His breath whistled in his nostrils and his belly wound up tight as he started toward the ridge, keeping low and moving fast. He'd nearly reached the base of the ridge when a craning head popped up against the stars. Magus forgot silence, yelled to waken the others and went up the ridge slope on the run, his blade before him.

Confused noise, cursing beyond the crest. Magus plowed past a blue bush, dodged around another and reached the summit. His right elbow bent backward. The sword blazed in the moonglare. He was ready to strike and kill the first Brother he saw—

Instead, he nearly ran himself onto three blades held in three quite human hands.

"Philosopher Lantzman!"

Arko Lantzman's sword hand shook a little. Ranged on either side of him were two of his bravos, their yellow boots pale against black broken rock. The bravo with the curling white scar on his chin gave Magus a thin, heartless smile and said: "Orders, Philosopher? Their camp's rousing. Shall we gut him and cut for it?"

"No, no," Lantzman said. The bravo looked disappointed.

Lantzman seemed shaken, uncertain. He licked his lips. The wind tossed his long graying hair and white beard. Above his reddened nose his brown eyes were moist.

"Your compassion surprises me," Magus growled. "And so does your presence here."

"William Catto is with you, isn't he?" Lantzman asked. Magus heard the anger in it.

"William Catto? I'm afraid I don't know—"

"No lies," Lantzman interrupted. "It's too late for lies and for a good deal else. The murdered authority was discovered in the drainage ditch an hour after your skysled took off. I knew you must have taken a stowaway. An inquiry at various inns proved it certain. William Catto"— Each time Lantzman said the name his childishly pink mouth twisted as though he tasted filth—"has vanished from his usual haunts. Did Catto force you to bring him?"

"No, if that's any of your affair," Magus replied.

On the plain boots hammered. The bravos moved wide to the left and right. The one with the chin scar chuckled low.

"As soon as it became evident that Catto was with you," Lantzman rushed on, "I knew I couldn't wait. I've spent too many years waiting already. At sunset, after you left, we broke into the government pool, killed authorities and stole a sled. At a price, at a price. I lost one of these good men to the government pikes."

"When did you land here?" Magus wanted to know.

"About half a day after you, I'd judge. We made six orbits before we risked touching down. I know a little about operating a sled. I used the scanning gear to fix on your own craft. We came down wide of the mark, reached your sled after a ten league march, and we've been following you since."

"Hoping, no doubt," said a voice from behind, "to kill us while we slept?"

Arko Lantzman's gaze slipped past Magus' shoulder. Once more there was revulsion, hatred greater than Magus could understand.

"Greeting, William Catto."

Red hair blazing, Catto strolled to the top of the ridge. He had his hand blaster cupped in his fist. The fact wasn't lost on the bravos. Even the one with the chin scar seemed less eager for a fight than he had a moment ago.

Quickly Magus explained to Catto about hearing the furtive noises and discovering Lantzman's party. He also reported that Lantzman had stolen a government sled.

"To follow me? Ah, that's true to pattern. Lantzman and I played bird-and-mouse for years. The Philosopher has been concerned that I might arrive on Lightmark ahead of him. As if that made any difference. You've set your rabbit's heart to beating for nothing, Lantzman." Catto's teeth glared in the moon as he smiled with all the charm of a skull. "I've always had the strongest claim. My grandfather was Prime Manager, yours only the Chief Philosopher. And my claim has one more advantage: I've got the guts to defend it. I'd suggest, Philosopher, that you and your bought bullies crawl away to your sled and consider yourself lucky to be alive. I mean to take Easkod for mine.''

"For filthy, dishonorable ends!" Lantzman cried. "To loot it. Strip it bare—"

"To make it *live* again!"

"To use it for your own profit!" Lantzman grew hysterical, spittle flying from his lips. "To make it the instrument of your robber's mentality—"

"You prating little slug!" Catto bawled back. "You pretend to such lofty motives. You'll be the liberator of Easkod, will you? In your selflessness you'll make the machines run again? The lights glow again? The automated lines produce again? The think-machines remember again? Just for the nobility of it? You're a liar, Philosopher Lantzman. You make me ill.''

"There's knowledge stored in Easkod, you barbaric filth. Knowledge that can bring II Galaxy back to life—"

Catto chucked. "Oratorical promises cost you nothing.

Suddenly Lantzman faced Magus. "He's a killer. You ought to be able to see that. You, girl—you're the wizard's daughter. I remember you. Make him listen.''

Only then did Magus understand that Robin and Maya had come up behind. Slurring his words, his swollen belly shaking, Arko Lantzman looked wild and somehow pitiable as he seized Magus' shoulders and shook him.

"Let the girl tell you, wizard! Surely she can recognize a man who'd kill for what he wants!"

Magus jerked away. "Are you much better, with your hired thugs?"

William Catto said, "Philosopher, it doesn't matter

a damn what these people think. I've traveled with them because it was expedient. I can continue to do so. But this—wizard—knows that he doesn't dare stand in my way.''

Magus' head whipped around. Expressionless, Catto ignored him. A little way down the shoulder of the ridge stood Maya, her cloak and russet hair flying out like banners in the night wind. Robin hunched beside her. His hand hung near his sword hilt. A muscle in his cheek worked and worked.

Arko Lantzman twisted his right hand under his cloak. He ripped at his doublet, pulled something out.

Little chain links flickered in the moon. The small metal cube hanging on the chain flashed like an eye.

''Perhaps no man here can stand in your way, Catto. But this can. This can.''

Catto seemed genuinely shaken. He started forward. The bravos thrust their swords up. Catto countered by leveling his hand blaster. Magus went rigid, ready to use his blade to protect Maya.

Then Catto checked. His eyes focused on the cube between the tips of Lantzman's fingers.

Lantzman giggled. ''I suppose you thought that because the Prime Manager's grandson didn't have them, the four original powering triggers were lost. Three were. Only three. I have the last one. My little philosopher's stone. Without it Easkod lies silent forever. All its lights, all its machines dead as they are now. As you well know, it takes this simple little control mechanism to start the whole plant functioning. Without this, Catto, without this you can stay on Lightmark for a century and Easkod will still be a ruin.''

High and lunatic, Lantzman's laugh chased up and

down the plain, echoing, echoing. Like some churl baiting a beast, the Philosopher dangled the cube at the end of the chain. He swung the chain to whirl the cube in a circle. Faster. Faster, until it dazzled into a single flashing circumference of light.

And he kept laughing.

For most of a minute William Catto didn't move. Around and around—

With one deep-voiced obscenity William Catto lost control. He brought his hand blaster up to firing position against his belly and charged the man with the tormenting laugh.

XIII

BEFORE MAGUS could react, someone reacted faster. A body hurled past him. Light flared on steel.

The tip of Robin's sword raked Catto's forearm. Catto spun, recognized his attacker, fired.

The sizzling ring of energy radiated from the weapon's muzzle, bathing the ridge crest with intense white light. Magus had only an instant to leap and strike Robin over with his rolled shoulder.

Both men went down, floundering. The energy ring passed over their heads. Magus rolled away, spitting shale and smelling ozone.

Lantzman called for his bodyguards to stand fast. William Catto didn't fire again. But there was fury on his long face as Magus scrambled up and stepped between him and Robin.

"I've done this before," Magus said in a harsh voice. "I'll keep doing it until you stop your private feud."

"I say it's time we settled—" Robin began.

"Gladly, whelp," Catto cut in. Blood on his bare forearm mingled with the thick mat of reddish hair. "I don't know what made you take Lantzman's side, a misplaced sense of justice or your overworked adolescent glands. But either way, I'll happily—"

Magus recoiled as Robin went tearing past him again.

Enraged, Magus seized Robin by the collar of his cloak and hammered his jaw with a balled fist. Robin cursed as the punch struck. He reeled back. Catto caught Robin's shoulder, spun him, kicked him in the seat of his breeches. Robin pitched down the ridge slope.

Catto grinned a wolf's grin, his long fingers tap-tapping on the butt of his blaster. Robin lurched to his feet. Apparently he'd twisted a muscle. As he started back up the slope his left leg folded beneath him and he fell.

Hating, Robin glared up at them from flat on his back.

Catto gestured with the hand blaster. "Stand up, boy. I can't kill you that way."

"No killing!" Magus roared. "Not unless you want to try me first."

"Provoke me a little more, wizard, and I might."

Then Catto got control of himself. A crooked grin slipped back onto his mouth. He shrugged as if to say he'd bow to Magus for the sake of expediency. But there was a new, distrustful dislike in his glance.

Catto shoved his hand blaster into his wide belt. He ripped off a strip of his cloak, wrapped it around his bleeding arm. He used his teeth to pull the knot tight.

Philosopher Lantzman nudged one of his bravos. "Help the lad up."

"But he's a friend of—"

"Help him up, I said."

The bravo slid down through the shale and gave

Robin a hand. A tense silence then closed down. Along the ridge dry blue leaves rasped as the wind stirred them.

Robin flung off the bravo's hand. His hurt leg bent under him. He bore the pain and stood unaided. White in the face, he called up the slope: "Perhaps I've discovered who my friends really are, Magus Blacklaw."

"Shut your mouth. You've caused enough trouble already. Put up your sword and let Maya look at your leg."

Robin didn't move.

"Do as I tell you, boy!"

"Go to hell. Nobody gives orders to a Dragonard."

William Catto doubled over laughing. Magus' heart nearly broke for the lad, young and brave and bawling his defiance in a way that came out comical. Robin turned from white to scarlet.

Magus turned to his daughter. Inexplicably, she too looked furious.

"Talk to him, Maya. Drive some sense into his head."

"No need for that," Robin called. "I'm leaving. I'll make my way alone."

"We'll go together, young man," Philosopher Lantzman said. "It seems I've found an ally." And he scuttled down the slope on his runty legs, his overweight belly bobbing.

The metal cube hanging from the neck chain glinted in the moonlight as Lantzman whispered in Robin's ear. A moment later Robin gave a quick nod. Lantzman laughed. He and Robin walked off across the dark plain stretching from the ridgeline.

Lantzman's two bravos fell in behind. They watched

Magus and Catto as they retreated. Slowly the four figures blended in with the darkness.

Catto reached for his blaster. "Better to kill them now before they come back to plague us."

Magus clamped fingers around the man's gun wrist. "Are you that much of an animal, Catto?"

The red haired man exhaled. "A hard question under the circumstances."

"I know the Philosopher has your little cube—"

"I'll get it."

"But can you commit four murders for it?"

Catto sighed. "No. I don't want to become a killer quite yet." Sardonic and more than a little serious, he squinted at Magus and added, "But beware the moment I do decide things have gone too far. Not all the pious sentiments in all the book-rolls in the universe will stop me from taking Easkod when the time comes."

"We can fight then if we have to."

"Agreed."

Magus let go of his arm. Catto walked away.

Now Magus diverted his attention to Maya. "Damnation, girl! Why are you crying?"

Her bitter sobs ripped out on the night wind. "You—just—don't—understand."

"I understand all too well that you're responsible for provoking Robin's outburst and his decision to abandon us. Listen to me! Stop howling like a lovelorn cat!" He gave her a shake. "If you hadn't made such a fuss over Catto—if you hadn't hung on his every word and ignored the lad—"

"I don't give a damn for Catto! It's Robin I love."

"*Robin!* I don't understand. You gave every sign it was otherwise—"

"That shows how much you know about women!" she wailed, hitting at his head with her fists. "If you didn't spend so much time with loose women, chasing after them like some carnal thing, you'd know more about real love."

It was as though she'd touched a deep, raw wound. "You arrogant little bitch, I loved your mother more than—"

She didn't hear. "Are you so simple that you couldn't see I was *trying* to make Robin jealous? Make him pay more attention to me? What was so wrong about that? Why can't you understand? *What kind of father are you?*"

Stunned, Magus watched her race off down the ridge slope, her russet hair streaming behind her. She disappeared in the dark around the cairn.

First Magus experienced flaming anger. He threw up his hands, marched back and forth swearing all the obscenities he knew, plus a few invented on the spot.

Then he grew ashamed for calling her the terrible names. Finally came confusion and despondency.

It helped not at all to remember that millions of other fathers, faced with the mysteries and paradoxes of a daughter's mind, must have felt equally frustrated and helpless in times past. No matter how ludicrous her outburst might seem to another, he knew he'd hurt her.

Well, wizard, you've botched this night magnificently. What next?

Next was Catto, waiting silently for him on the plain. As he returned wearily to the cairn, Magus came upon him with a start.

"Before we try to sleep again," Catto said, "one question."

"Yes?"

"What do you want on Lightmark?"

"To finish my mission. To get free of the clutches of the Governors so I can go back to Pastora and live without being hounded. To do that I have to exorcise the demons."

"But we both know the exorcism business is a lie. You've no magic powers."

Magus' eyes hardened. "The Governors don't know it. If you're thinking about trying to steal this"—he touched the wafer at his throat—"so you can tell them, we'll fight sooner than I anticipated."

"No, your situation with the Governors is your affair. Now tell me what you really want."

"Enough apparatus from Easkod City to bring me comfortable money. I plan to smuggle them back to Pastora and sell them."

"Illegally?"

"What other way is there?"

Catto's delight at discovering cupidity showed. "All right. I can spare them to you, I suppose."

"I mean to take them whether you say you can spare them or not."

Catto chuckled. "Very well. But you should be just as clear about my intentions. I mean to have all of Easkod for myself. There's been serious trouble tonight. There will be more if I find you in my way."

"I understand."

"Good," Catto said. He turned and loped long-strided back to the cairn.

Magus sat among the rocks long into the night, brooding, sleepless.

Robin gone out there in the windy waste with Philosopher Lantzman.

Maya hating him; he could hear her sobbing when the wind was right.

And Catto growing more defiant by the hour.

Sighing, Magus rose. He walked a few steps onto the plain and stared into the black north. The towers of Easkod City gleamed a ghostly silver.

I'm certainly reaching the end of my resources as a wizard, he thought with some bitterness. *Soon I'll have to call on my resources as a man. I wonder if they're adequate, for surely there's worse ahead.*

In that he proved a most accurate prophet.

XIV

A MUSTY WIND blew out of the north as they made their way toward Easkod at first light.

Maya said only the things absolutely necessary to get them started, breaking off the sticky blocks of nutrient and passing them around. They ate as they walked. Magus noticed her chewing on one block and holding another in her left hand as they leaned into the wind. He realized she'd broken a block for Robin without thinking.

He fell back a step or so, watching. Maya finished her block. She lifted the other and stared at it a moment. With a little sob she threw it away into the shale.

He caught up with her. "Maya—"

"There's nothing to be said, Father."

From the way she said it, he might have been a stranger. She wrapped her cloak higher around her throat and the lower part of her face. Her violet eyes blazed in sideways glances of—anger? sorrow? contempt? All three. Then she hurried ahead.

Walking became more difficult as the wind increased. Tiny particles of shale stung against his cheeks. Soon his nostrils and eyelids and mouth clogged. He leaned forward, wrapping his cloak around his nose and mouth as Maya had done.

At sunrise Graphos had been visible as a murky disk. Now it had vanished in a thick, tawny haze. Visibility was limited to a short distance.

Gradually the three adjusted their own speeds and drew closer together for mutual protection. The sullen tan light filled the world. The wind gibbered and screamed, falling off one moment, buffeting them the next. Already Magus felt the physical strain of walking against that blast for an extended time.

"It's growing worse," he shouted. "We ought to find cover."

"There isn't any," Catto yelled back.

Magus discovered it was true. He'd been concentrating so hard on the way directly ahead, he'd failed to notice that they had reached the apex of the V-shaped plain and passed beyond the protection of the flanking ridges. They were on a much broader plain now, one where only widely scattered cairns hulked in the blowing murk. The plain sloped upward toward the boiling dust obscuring the whole northern half of the horizon.

"Either we turn back or we go ahead and find cover at Easkod," Catto bawled. "I vote for the latter. We can't be too far now."

Magus nodded. They bore on into the windstorm.

Another few minutes and walking became even more difficult. The plain here was sandy. Magus sank halfway to the tops of his boots. Maya foundered at every step. Even Catto moved slowly.

The wind thrust harder. All of Magus' exposed skin long ago had caked with a yellowish goo compounded of dust and sweat. Catto was barely discernible three strides ahead.

Odd how the deepening brown light tricked vision. There seemed to be a shadow of a man just to the left of Catto. Even as Magus peered, it vanished behind a fresh puff of dust.

Hallucination, Magus said to himself. *We'll go blind and out of our heads before long.*

His chest ached. Breathing hurt. All at once he realized he'd lost track of Maya. He stopped, then turned in a full circle.

"Maya? Maya!"

The wind threw the sound back and whirled it around him.

Mayamayamayamaya–

Panic seized him. "Catto, I've lost Maya!" Ahead the red-haired man shouted something that the wind turned to gibberish. Magus circled again, calling his daughter's name over and over. The echoes sprang back at him, overlapping. *Mayamayamayamaya-maya—*

A faint cry. Somewhere to his left. Magus ran in that direction.

Abruptly the dust-whirl thickened, then parted like a curtain being ripped. He saw her, indistinct but recognizable, not ten paces off. Her cloak snapped out behind her like a dark flag. She weaved on her feet, pressing her hands up to shield her eyes.

"Over here, Maya! Hold on, I'm coming!"

She heard him but the wind tricked her. She turned away from him, hands held out, searching. Catto caught up with Magus then.

And they both saw the Brother in the dust behind her, a sharp-studded club in his right hand.

The dust blotted out the apparition.

"Did you see it?" Magus cried.

"Aye." Catto dug beneath his cloak for his hand blaster. "A minute ago I thought I saw something moving close by me, but with the sand blowing so hard—" Catto bit off his words, swung the blaster muzzle like a pointer. "I think they're circling us. Using the storm's cover—look there!"

Magus saw Maya again. A Brother ran at her, club raised.

Magus bolted forward. Maya saw the creature coming, dodged away, struck at it with her fist. Magus jerked out his blade.

He reached the girl, threw her around behind him. *Scree-scree* sang the wordless voice of the Brother sidling toward him with club held high. *Scree-scree*—another one materialized beside the first.

Six appeared in the murk to his left.

Six more on the right.

Eight ahead.

Ten behind.

Each Brother wore a transparent membrane-like hood that completely covered his head. The hoods were cinched tightly to their throats by thongs, and in the front center of each one, tiny circular grids gleamed.

Breathing vents? Likely. The Brother moved with little difficulty in the pummeling storm.

Slowly the creatures closed the ring around the three. And then a Brother taller than the rest glided out of the murk. A scaly crest thrust up from the top of his forehead, running all the way over the top of his skull and down the back of his neck. He raised his own huge, studded club, brought it down in a pointing signal.

"That must be their leader, Plume," Magus cried. Sword up, he charged them.

Scree-scree-scree. Magus slid in fast beneath a club aimed at his head. He drove his sword through a transparent hood into a creature's mouth.

The blade shuddered as it struck hard tissue. He jerked the sword loose, smelling vile ooze. The creature fell.

Clubs hammered his shoulders. He gored the guts of another creature, cropping it. Two more clubs bounced off his left ribs, right temple. The Brothers pressed all around, making that damnable high-pitched cry. A spear ripped toward his belly.

Magus jackknifed backward. He collided with a Brother, whirled, lunged aside. The second Brother screamed as the spear of the first sank into his belly.

A few paces off, Catto was down. Two Brothers beat him with clubs. His blaster had fallen from his fingers, lay half covered by blown dust. Magus dived for it, shifting his sword to his left hand. He sprawled on his belly and got hold of the weapon. On his knees, he fumbled with the triggering grip.

Four Brothers converged, the awesome figure of Plume right behind, tall as a god. Under Plume's transparent hood immense distended eyes glared. The first of the four was almost on him. Magus fired.

A widening ring of white light ate its way toward the Brothers. Their hoods lit up with an eerie brilliance, flared blindingly on contact. Hideous shrieks drowned in a bubbling and crackling of scarlet hide. A second later nothing was left but smoking remains: a leg, a chunk of torso, a splintered club. The stormy air smelled unclean.

Brother Plume had escaped the blast. He was circling swiftly to the right. He joined another group of Brothers moving in more warily. Magus fired again.

Another white ring. Another flash. The dying *scree*.

He heard a cold, pleased laugh at his shoulder. "Give it to me. Let me take a few of the bastards."

Catto wrenched the weapon away, ran to the left and shot. Three more Brothers disintegrated.

Brother Plume was a fierce but prudent leader. He exhorted his followers with high-pitched, unintelligible commands. But he managed to avoid the killing light of the blaster, melting away from his followers to let them die, appearing a moment later with another band.

Catto turned a hundred and eighty degrees. More Brothers coming at them. Magus took a blow of a club on the back of his head. He fended a spear thrust with his bare fist. Catto dropped to one knee, fired.

This close, the energy-ring flared backward after it seared the Brothers. Catto knocked Magus to the ground. The white backwash passed over their heads in tangible waves of heat.

Light spots dazzled the back of Magus' eyes as he clawed his way to his feet. He swung his head, searching. A trip-hammer of terror beat inside his chest.

"She's gone, Catto. I don't see her anywhere."

The dust thickened. A few Brothers drifted behind it, circling but not charging. Magus spied Plume, ran toward him. He foundered in the shifting sand.

A Brother glided up beside the leader, spoke, pointing away. Plume's hooded head bobbed twice. He saluted Magus mockingly with his huge studded club. Then he melted into the storm.

"They've gone, Catto! *They've taken her—!*"

Fear drove him out of his mind.

He lunged like a lunatic, back and forth through the dust, crying her name. He flung his sword away, cupped crusted hands to his gritty mouth, shouted her name over and over. Little echoes of it crisscrossed around him like threads in a fabric.

Mayamayamayamaya–

A hand caught him. Snarling like a rabid animal, Magus batted it aside.

"Let loose! I'm going after her."

"We can't afford to get separated, Magus. We'll search together."

For one piercing instant Magus wondered what sort of man William Catto really was. A compassionate killer? He tossed the riddle away, the pain of losing Maya consuming him.

Catto added his voice to the search. The echoes grew more tangled.

MayaMAYA.

MayaMAYA.

MAYAMAYA!

They blundered in circles for the better part of an hour. The blowing dust paled to beige. Then it began to settle as the wind died.

Magus faced the empty plain. His sword dragged from his right hand. His face was a filthy mask of sweat and dust. The silver towers of Easkod had reappeared, lying but a league or so to the north now, beyond a final barrier ridge.

Catto hailed him from that direction. Magus staggered toward him. Catto pointed down at disturbed shale and something else that stank.

"Here's where they must have picketed the beasts. Look at all the droppings."

Catto's moustaches ruffled in the wind. He pointed up the plain.

"You see where they took her. Probably it's their stronghold."

Hurting as he'd never hurt before, Magus followed the path of Catto's finger. The beast-trails marking the retreat of the Brothers led straight up and over the last ridge, to Easkod City.

XV

LESS THAN AN HOUR LATER, Magus and Catto crossed the final ridge and descended the gently sloping plain toward the silver towers.

The air had cleared after the storm. Visibility was excellent. The towers seemed to leap toward the sky with frozen grace. As Hans Huygens had said, no trace of age marred them: no smears of mold or patches of rust. The wind still blew from the north. As it swept along down the wide boulevards it picked up an eerie note, exactly as though a soprano voice sang a sad counterpoint.

Some of the old superstitious dread gripped Magus as they marched on steadily toward that beautiful, silent monument to a lost age. He was staggered by the very number and complexity of the structures. He counted at least two hundred.

From a distance only the silver spires had been visible. Now Magus saw the other lower buildings that spread out horizontally between tower bases. Some were silver domes. Others were spheres that stood on silver stilt-legs a story above ground, connected by silver pipes.

This piping ran from building to building, ten, twenty, thirty pipes held together by massive silver bands to form a multiple conduit that soared, dipped, changed direction a dozen times before it disappeared into one of the structures. There were hundreds of such networks of massed pipes, mostly strung two stories above ground.

Between the individual structures and below the pipes the two men glimpsed small arid parks. On the broad avenues pinkish creepers had thrust up through the earth to overturn many of the paving blocks. Only these wasted little parks and ruined roads testified to the passage of time in Easkod City.

The size of the place staggered Magus most of all. Many of the low domes covered an area equivalent to thirty squares in any town on Pastora. The working population of Easkod must have numbered in the millions once.

William Catto walked silently beside him. On his face was an expression of ravenous joy. He touched his companion's sleeve and pointed into the singing wind.

"See that tallest tower? There in the center? That would be the most important building."

A meager nod from Magus. True, the tower Catto indicated was impressive. It stood far taller than the rest. But Magus was again concentrating on the tracks they'd been following. The tracks led directly to the beginning of a broad avenue just ahead. Magus said: "It's a big place to search."

Catto scratched his red moustaches. "Aye."

"We'll search it till we find her. That is, I will. You've other things on your mind, haven't you?"

"Many other things. But I have no doubt the

Brothers will be waiting for us somewhere ahead. We may find them—and your daughter—without too much effort. After all, we're about to desecrate their holy place.'' He was grinning his wolf's grin.

The singing wind beat around Magus' head as they started on. Already Graphos was falling. The light slanted. Shadows thickened around the silver bases of the spires. Magus thought about reporting back to Pastora via the throat-wafer.

Disgusted, he rejected the idea. The time for mummery had passed. The High Governors could sit listening to silence the rest of their dessicated lives for all he cared. Only Maya mattered now.

Catto's whisper jolted him out of his reverie. ''Don't turn, Magus. Just slide your eyes to the left. Out on the plain there's a cairn about half a league away. I think I saw a man there.''

Stopping, Magus pretended to adjust the thong at the top of his jackboot. He peered up through his eyebrows, noted the distant isolated cairn. Sure enough, he spotted the silhouette of a head. Then three more. He caught a flash of yellow hair. He stood up.

''Philosopher Lantzman. And he and his friends are making no secret of watching us either. Not a one's moved back into cover. Why pretend we don't see them?'' He turned full in the direction of the cairn.

Catto shielded his eyes. ''Wanting to let us enter Easkod first, are they? So we can be the bait for the Brothers? Nice of them.''

Magus thought of Robin. He made a decision. ''I'm going to parley with them.''

''Parley! What in the name of hell for?''

''Six men together will be safer than two in Easkod City.''

"Throw in with Lantzman? No thank you. I'll have nothing to do with that—"

"Then stay here, damn you. It's my daughter's life I'm concerned about, not your personal battle for authority over this graveyard!"

Magus spun and started walking toward the cairn. He'd gone only a few steps when Catto called.

"I can promise you'll get no help from them. . . ." The wind blew the rest away.

Magus bit off the distance with long, ferocious strides. He detected activity in the cairn. Two heads bobbed out of sight. They reappeared at the opposite side of the rocks a moment later. The bravos. Magus eased his sword hilt free. He kept walking.

By the time he reached the cairn all the watchers had vanished. He stopped. He raised his left hand palm up in the universal peace symbol.

Silence. The wind picked at the shale.

"Lantzman? I want to talk. Tell your thugs they can put their swords away."

A tangly gray head poked up. "All right, you can approach. But make sure your own sword's put away too."

Magus bobbed his head to signify acceptance. Lantzman came cautiously into the open. Robin appeared on a ledge higher up on the cairn. He jumped down to the ground as the bravos glided from hiding, their yellow boots bright against the dun earth. The one with the scar on his chin watched Magus closely. His thumb was hooked on his belt near his dagger.

Magus said, "You've evidently been following us so perhaps you know that during the storm this morning, the creatures struck us again."

Lantzman's face remained blank. His pudgy fingers

fiddled with the cube on the neck-chain. Robin was just behind him, gold eyes not quite meeting Magus' own. Magus knew without being told that Lantzman and the others were aware of the attack.

Lantzman's mouth puckered, sour. "Since you and Catto are still traveling together, I presume it's by choice. Consequently I have no interest in—"

"We were thrown together by accident. Say this for him: he tried to help when the Brothers carried off my daughter."

Robin gasped.

"Didn't you wonder why you didn't see her with us, Robin?"

"Yes. But I thought you might have sent her back to the sled."

"They carried her off. She's in the city if she's not dead by now. To answer you, Lantzman, I don't care about Catto's plans for Easkod. Nor about yours. I'm concerned about Maya. The Brothers are probably waiting in the city, hiding, planning another attack. We'll all stand a better chance if we go in together. I propose we join forces."

One of the bravos snickered. Magus' pulse picked up a beat. Redness swam behind his eyes. He controlled it.

Philosopher Lantzman seemed pleased to be approached in this way. He thought over the request, running a finger down his beard. But finally he shook his head.

"I'll beg you if that's what you want," Magus said.

"The answer is still no. Go your own way with Catto."

"What happens to the girl is no affair of yours, eh?"

"You have it wrong, wizard. I gave you every opportunity to join me. And I recall that back at the New

Brussels Steamhouse, I was the one doing the begging. My plea was turned down flat. You've sided with Catto since your arrival on Lightmark. To finish what I meant to say when you interrupted me, I have no interest in what happens to you. If that implies that I have no interest in your daughter, so be it.''

A muscle wrenched in Magus' jaw. ''Greed takes precedence over humanity?''

Lantzman's ravaged face shone ugly in the sunlight. ''If you expected otherwise, wizard, you're a fool. I've spent all my life waiting for this moment. And frankly, I suspect your little story is a fraud. Very likely Catto has turned your head by telling you he'll share the wealth of Easkod. Persuaded you to hide your daughter, try to trap me into cooperation. It won't work.'' Lantzman licked his lips and touched the little cube on its chain. ''I still have this, remember. I intend to keep it for my own.''

Hate rose thick in Magus' throat. He turned slightly.

''Will you lend us your sword again, Robin?''

''I—''

Robin looked out past Magus' blowing cloak to where Catto waited. His gold eyes hardened. He shook his head. He turned and walked swiftly back to the cairn.

A deep sense of failure overwhelmed Magus then. He knew he'd come close to persuading the lad. But jealousy and the memory of humiliation had won out.

Philosopher Lantzman was whistling. Magus moved away. The voice of one of the bravos cracked out behind him:

''I hope you find the wench. Then when the Philosopher bids us kill you—provided the Brothers don't handle it first—we'll leave her alive.''

Magus swung back. It was the scar-chinned bravo who'd spoken. His lips curled, nasty. "I took a fancy to her looks, wizard. I'd like to peel off her cloak and see her pretty—"

Magus charged, breaking the bravo's nose with his balled fist.

Blood squirted. The bravo went down, thrashing, swearing obscenely.

Magus watched the fallen man a moment. Then he turned away, started once more toward where Catto was standing against the backdrop of the silver city.

A clatter of boots. A startled cry from Lantzman. The bravo's dagger was a sun-bright shard flashing for Magus' eyes.

Magus wrenched aside. The dagger caught his cheek, tearing flesh, bringing blood. By that time Magus had his sword drawn. He rammed it into the side of the bravo's neck, driving it on out the other side. There was a madness of hate and of frustration on him. He hauled the sword out. The bravo fell. Magus skewered his ribs, his belly, his throat again.

The sword came free with a final twist. Magus kicked shale in the bravo's face. Lantzman and the other bravo were too stunned to move. Robin's face showed a hundred agonies and indecisions.

Magus cursed himself. A scant second ago there had still been a chance of help from Lantzman. If things got bad enough and the Philosopher felt the fury of an attack by the Brothers he might have changed his mind. Now there was no chance at all.

Magus' cloak belled around him as he stepped over the dead bravo. Fat carrion bugs already crawled in the shining blood on the slashed throat.

Small against the immensity of Easkod's towers and the Lightmark plain, Magus and Catto came together and turned their faces north. The men at the cairn watched.

When the two of them reached the city's edge Magus glanced back.

The cairn was deserted.

He hurried to catch up with Catto, passing from slanting daylight into the first chill shadow between the silver buildings.

XVI

THE ATTACK came just at sunset that same day, on a broad avenue deep in the corporate city.

The two men had been exploring for several hours. The things they saw astonished Magus and delighted William Catto.

They explored a silver dome occupying an area the equivalent of six city squares. In it they discovered a maze of serpentine tracks. The tracks were made of light metal rollers. Square metal towers rose among the tracks at various points around the dome's floor. A typical tower was faced with hundreds of thousands of tiny hemispherical lights, all dark. Rows of colored levers jutted from each tower, just in front of a sculptured seat built out from one face of the square about halfway to the top.

"An automatic production plant," Catto said. But when he tried to describe the complex optical goods the plant produced (the descriptions were based on what he remembered of stories handed down from his grandfather the Prime Manager) Magus was lost.

In one of the spires they entered, four lower floors comprised a gloomy rotunda. Immense convex disks of glass were ranged around the walls inside transparent display bubbles.

"This building was an optics research center, very likely," Catto said.

In a mammoth shed-like building they saw ten-story vats of a coppery metal. The vats were suspended high above in wire cradles. Multiple pipes by the thousands converged upon the building, came through the walls and wove a motionless labyrinth below and above and around the onion-shaped vessels. Catto explained that this area probably had something to do with chemical synthesis required in producing light-sensitive materials for image formation: "Soul-pictures, as you call them, eh?"

Catto was like a child given a bottomless bag of sweets. He laughed and talked constantly as he led Magus from place to place. Magus had trouble paying attention. He was on the lookout for signs of Maya or the Brothers.

Such signs were almost nonexistent. They did come across the print of a horny foot in the dust of one of the arid little parks. That was all.

The twilight settled. Catto suggested a pause for something to eat before they took up their search again. They were on a ruined avenue that ran through the heart of the city. At the avenue's end the tallest tower shot to the sky.

Halfway up its façade great yellow letters stood out from the surface, brilliant in the waning day: CORPORATION OF EASKOD.

Magus unshipped his skimpy pack. Dispiritedly he set about chewing a gummy block of nutrient. Catto bit into his own food with glee.

"We'll find her, don't worry," Catto said between mouthfuls. "I still have this." He tapped the hand blaster.

"Yes, but if they've harmed her, if it's already too late . . ." Magus shook his head.

They were sitting on the edge of a ruined fountain in the center of the avenue. Its parabolic dish cast a shadow over them. Magus swallowed the last of his nutrient. In the act of wiping his hands on his breeches he glanced up. He froze.

"Yonder, Catto. Other side of the avenue. Behind that piping. I'm sure I saw—"

Before Catto could reply, the *scree-scree* chorus began.

Magus hauled out his sword. Catto pulled the blaster. From a little park near the pipes to which Magus had referred a band of Brothers rushed. Similar bands broke out of cover at other points along the avenue.

Seeming almost relaxed, Catto knelt behind the fountain's edge. He took aim, fired. The sizzling white ring spread. The Brothers charging from the park scattered. The energy blast diffused harmlessly.

Magus gnawed his lip, waiting for the creatures to close so he could use his sword. In that instant, the first of the attackers held up a new, unfamiliar weapon.

The weapon consisted of a short black wand carried vertically. At the top was a translucent teardrop-shaped bulb twice as big as a man's fist. All the Brothers had these devices, Magus saw. They ran at the fountain with the devices held out in front of them.

Catto took aim again. One of the wand devices flashed. The furiously white light spread around the two men instantly. Magus was blinded.

The air sang with the faint hiss of more bulb-wands

lighting. Magus blinked, but the whorls of white on his retinas threw everything into dappled confusion. Catto shot. The popping lights made him miss.

The Brothers raced toward the fountain. Their bulb-lights kept flashing, flashing, flashing—

"I can't see, Catto!" Magus flailed around him with his sword. The Brothers were very close.

"It's some kind of auxiliary light source. They had such in the olden times for—"

Catto cried out in pain. There were sounds of struggle.

Magus hacked the air with his sword, two hands on the hilt. He struck nothing. Yet he was conscious of the advance of the creatures all around him.

Flash, flash, flash.

Magus lashed the air with his sword. He knew the Brothers were dodging away from its hacking tip. The inside of his head flamed with afterimages. Somewhere Catto let out another gargantuan roar. Maddened, Magus plunged at the lights again.

Flash, flash, flash, flash.

Magus threw an arm across his eyes and screamed in pain.

Chitinous hands seized his waist, wrists, legs. His sword was torn from his fingers. He was lifted. The stink of the hide of the Brothers gagged him.

Flash, flash, flash.

The hands hurled him hard against the parabolic fountain.

He struck and slid to the pavement. All the lights went out.

His tongue tasted of dirt and his head ached fiercely as he came dizzying back to consciousness.

Scaly hands held him fast. He was pulled to his feet. He smelled the smell of alien bodies as he opened his eyes and found himself captive inside a ring of the Brothers near the dried-up fountain.

At close range the faces of the creatures were even more hideous than he recalled. Their swollen white hemispheres of eyes glistened with the immense black pupils. One band of Brothers held Magus. Directly across the way a similar group had Catto. He'd sustained a vicious forehead wound. It leaked blood into his right eye and down his cheek.

A larger circle of Brothers completely enclosed the prisoners and their guards. In the center, equidistant from both captives, stood the tallest and fiercest of all the things.

His white-and-black eyes fixed first on Catto, then on Magus. There was a certain majestic authority about him. His spiny crest, running from the centerpoint of his forehead over his head and down between his shoulder scales, was etched against the towers and the fading sky.

"Plume." The tall creature pronounced the word with a faint clicking of the slit-like mouth. "Keeper of the holy of holies, this place. You come to desecrate. It cannot be."

"Where's my daughter?" Magus demanded. "Where's the girl you took?"

"In our place. Our holding place."

"Is she alive or dead?"

Slowly Plume nodded.

"Yes, the female desecrator. Alive. Until." There was a threat in the final word.

Catto tried to sound bold, full of bluff. "Let us go.

You've got no claim on this place. It belongs to human-kind. Maybe you were part of that once. You aren't any longer."

"Holy Easkod is our place," Plume said. "You come out of the stars in something which does not travel on the land. You must be evil. Brothers travel only on the land. You come to desecrate. Holy Easkod is our place."

"Yes, yes. Our place. Our place," echoed a hundred slit-mouths.

How to communicate with them? How to make them understand or fear? Magus despaired.

What few traces of physical humanity were left —their bi-ped form, their eye-and-mouth faces—had been submerged by the changes worked on them by the nuclear rains. Yet they retained traces of human guile. They had been clever enough to wear protective hoods in the storm, and to use the ancient wand lights as weapons.

Catto gnawed his lips, tried again by pointing at Magus.

"That man—he is a worker of magic."

Plume remained impassive.

"He can summon demons to his bidding. He can destroy demons too. Your demons."

A few of the Brothers hissed, waving their bulb-wands.

Catto grinned a desperate grin. "That's right! He's not afraid of you."

"Then," said Plume, "let there be testing of the magic."

Catto's mouth dropped open. Plume went on:

"Let you be sent one by one to the abode of the

magic of Easkod. No Brother goes there. It is forbidden. Even Plume cannot go. But desecrators will go. First the wizard. There he shall stand and pit his magic against the holy magic we guard.''

Magus' lips felt parched. "Go where?"

"Hauntplace."

And all the old terror flooded back.

Magus remembered the dying tale of Hans Huygens. Though he struggled against it, his reason submerged beneath a crawling fear black as the lowering night.

Brother Plume pointed his lightwand at Magus' waist. Finally Magus realized the meaning of the gesture.

"My sword? What about it?"

"Is that the wand of your magic?"

When Magus nodded Plume did likewise.

"That you may take to the Hauntplace. Nothing more."

Then Plume let out a single, sharp cry. The Brothers cried *scree-scree* and closed around Magus, battering at his head.

He punched, kicked, fought them. They were too many. He went down.

He felt himself being raised on many chitinous hands. As the accumulated effects of the punishment he'd taken replaced sense with darkness in his mind, they carried him off to the Hauntplace.

XVII

"Tell us your name. Tell us your name, your name."

The whispering penetrated darkness, struck to the core of Magus' just-waking mind.

At first he thought only one voice asked the insistent question. Then he grew conscious of several speaking in unison.

He groaned. He moved his eyelids against the dark. Sensory signals poured in from all parts of his body. A gentle heat on the back of his neck, as from the mild rays of a sun. Coarse grassy stuff tickling his outflung hands, his right cheek.

He lay facedown. He ached from the beating by the Brothers. His ears began to differentiate more selectively. He still heard the repeated question. It seemed to come from directly above. But he heard other noises as background. Wind rustling foliage. The murmur of surf. Raucous animal cries, honkings and snortings that sounded curiously like magnified electronic tones. A growl reverberated.

"Tell us your name, your name."

Panic clutched Magus in a hard hand. He remembered that he'd been condemned to the Hauntplace.

He fought to overcome the runaway fear. He mastered it, thrust it down to a controllable level. He levered himself up on his palms and opened his eyes.

Long aquamarine grass rippled ahead of him. It stretched to the lip of a promontory. The face of the promontory dropped away to a foaming butter-colored ocean beneath a sky just changing from scarlet to orange.

Out near the horizon the sky held a peculiar distortion, as though it curved around to embrace the sea and promontory on both sides. He could not be certain.

Magus slid his hand down along his ribs. He touched the commonplace metal of the hilt of his sword. He felt a little better.

He'd never seen such supersaturated colors in sea or sky or land anywhere in his life. At the moment his surroundings didn't strike him as especially hostile. But the color scheme was unnatural enough to start him worrying.

Had the Brothers drugged him? Was the Hauntplace some kind of induced hallucination? He struggled to his feet. He pinched his arm. Solid as ever. Except for the lingering pains from the beating he didn't feel too badly. Surely he'd be light-headed or dazed if he were under drugs.

But if the Hauntplace wasn't in his own mind, where was it? No such topography existed on Lightmark, of that he was fairly certain.

"Tell us your name. Tell us your name."

The sky changed from orange to indigo. He swung around toward the source of the voices.

His eyes widened in horror as he tried to comprehend the things rearing above him, ten times as tall as he was.

A small forest of stalk-like plants confronted him. Their saffron trunks rose to a considerable height before branching. At the ends of about half of the branches hung bare human eyeballs with pupils of red, purple, amber, emerald green. The pupils functioned. They enlarged, adjusting to the deepening color of the sky.

On the remaining stalks, pink orifices shaped like human mouths spoke to him:

"Tell us your name."

His palms sweated. He was trapped here on the promontory. The only possible escape lay straight ahead through the stalks with their swaying branches.

The mouths spoke in unison, sounding angry.

"Your name!"

Magus started forward.

The branches whipped down toward him. The glistening eyeballs and wet pink mouths were only a hand's width above him.

"Tell us your name, your name!"

Magus dodged along beneath the thrashing branches as they pressed lower. He bent double to avoid their touch. Grotesquely large, a stalked eyeball swung down directly in front of him.

Magus thrust his sword into the pupil. The steel sliced through nothingness.

The eyeball hovered above him. Could the stalk have retracted so quickly that he failed to see it? Impossible. Yet his sword had penetrated only empty air.

Blinking, Magus shook his head and hurried on. The voices hissed angrily.

"Your name, your name. You must tell us your name!"

Safely through the bizarre plants, Magus halted again. Terror plucked at him. His heart worked heavily inside his chest. He felt ridiculously puny. He wished he possessed some authentic magical powers.

Ahead, the aquamarine grass swept to a hilltop crowned by a glade of immense flowers. The stems of the flowers were so thick no human could have reached around them. High against the shifting sky at the tip of each stem gigantic umbrella petals tossed in the wind, raining fist-size puffs of iridescent pollen.

There was no question of standing fast. Surely somewhere in this madness of exaggerated form and color, he'd find something which smacked of sanity or signified a way of escape. If he let himself believe otherwise he'd go out of his mind.

He climbed the hill toward the flowers.

He walked through a shower of the pollen-puffs. He reached out to grasp one. Somehow it eluded him and he held onto emptiness again. He cursed, kept moving.

All at once the sky went pitch black. A thousand suns appeared, spreading across the whole curved canopy above him. They radiated visible spokes of light. Suddenly one of the suns fell.

Magus' face lit up with the blooming brilliance. The fireball filled his vision, falling directly upon the spot where he stood. He even imagined he felt its heat as it loomed—

The sun plunged past the promontory to crash into the yellow ocean with a thunderous roar. Gigantic waves rolled as the ball of burning gas disappeared beneath the surface. Steam clouds rose. They trailed out on the wind, engulfed the promontory, swept around Magus on the hillside.

When the clouds had boiled away the sky shone bone-white, as on a misty morning.

Cold sweat ran down his cheeks into his beard. He swallowed hard, started into the maze of flower stems.

When he'd worked his way through about half the thicket, he had reservations about proceeding further. The view beyond the flowers looked even more forbidding.

A dank ferny wood ran as far as he could see on either hand. Its interior drifted with steam. Magus walked out of the flowers as the sky changed to a shade of copper like a stormy sunset.

His right boot came down next to something that made a wet sound.

A transparent tentacle with thread-like red tubes running through it rose out of a large hole in the ground barring his path. Inside the thread-tubes miniscule bubbles flowed.

He took a step back as another arm twisted up to link with the first. More and more arms appeared. They rose vertically, then they shot out at oblique angles to touch and twine around one another. Soon several dozen of the monstrosities had exuded themselves, interlaced to form a slimy mesh that prevented any forward passage.

Magus let his eyes slide leftward. He figured he could run in that direction, around the end of the web that was busily weaving itself into ever more intricate loops. He moved with sudden speed.

Before he took six steps the entire mass of intertwined tentacles shifted. He was again caught behind the wall. The red fluid bubbled fiercely through the little thread-tubes. The tentacles glowed a deep green as the sky changed.

Balked, Magus tried a run to the right. Once more the wall shifted. Now rage made him reckless. Gripping his sword, he ran straight at the shuddering mass.

The interwoven arms fell toward him like a collapsing building. A shriek ripped unbidden from his mouth. He hacked blindly—

Only to find he was cutting emptiness again.

Strand by strand, the tentacle-wall pulled itself rapidly back into the hole. No tentacle showed damage. yet Magus was certain he'd cut into the seething mass.

The sky turned yellow. Ragged gray thunderclouds sped into sight over the giant flowers. The last tentacle retracted. The hole sealed itself, the aquamarine turf extending inward on all sides, *growing* the hole closed.

"Out of my mind, that's it," Magus muttered. "This place has done it."

To test the conclusion he pricked his other palm with the tip of his sword.

Pain. A tiny jewel of blood appeared.

He wiped his hand on his tunic. His senses were still working. But he felt less sure of himself with each passing second. Less confident of his own ability to hang onto his mental balance.

If this were induced hallucination, how in hell's name could he be so acutely conscious? He'd felt the bite of his sword.

Then why did it have no effect on the horrors all around?

Had the Brothers somehow bewitched his sword? Rendered it powerless?

That must be it. Yet his reason told him that such demonic powers didn't exist.

How could he be so sure? He was in the Hauntplace.

A raw cry struggled up in his throat. He turned and stumbled toward the dank woods. He had to find an escape hatch, be it a real one or only the blessing of unconsciousness—

Of death. As he ran he realized how deeply this nightmare world was affecting him. Death seemed desirable. A balm, a boon.

Before he reached the steaming forest a deep rhythmic thudding began in its depths. It pounded at the bone of his head, brought a piercing pain between his eyes. Suddenly he saw small spherical creatures covered with sticky scintillant hairs whizzing around his boots.

They came bounding at him from all quarters. he kicked at one, thought he felt a glutinous contact but couldn't be sure. He wasn't sure of anything now.

The sticky hairballs bounced around him a minute more, then went whizzing away as the sky turned milky. Bolts of lightning began to flicker and sizzle.

The thundering out of the dank forest grew louder. Magus imagined he felt the earth shaking under his boots. Something was coming. Something was charging out of the forest, driving clouds of fantastic insects with glowing antennae and wings the hue of lampflame ahead of it.

A shining haze of insects flashed past his head. Thunder reverberated in the sky. The red lightnings crackled. The wind picked up, bending the flower-trees into agonized bows.

A bird with a wingspread three times greater than the reach of his arms flapped past him. Four green crystals in its squarish head radiated light. The dank forest shook, rustled, screamed with deafening life. Creatures pink and purple, oval and spindly, bass-voiced and reed-pitched, came rolling and flying and galloping at him in frantic retreat from whatever it was thundering and thundering out of the wood.

Magus chewed down on his bottom lip again. This time blood ran.

A heart of darkness appeared in the wood's center.

The terrified forest creatures sailed past him, shrieking, chittering, bellowing, croaking. The red lightnings flashed. Thunder pealed.

Stand fast, Magus Blacklaw. You've survived this much without a mark.

Yet he knew otherwise. The marks had been left on his crumbling mind.

Out of the dank forest burst the earth-shaker. Magus choked.

The mammoth four-footed monster waved its long, flexible snout. There were four tusks to either side of its jaw. Witless amber eyes shone from its slab head. Lightning illuminated its dappled white and gray flanks. They heaved in and out as the thing snorted, drowning the thunder. It slammed the earth with huge horny feet, running straight toward Magus.

A bolt of red lightning crashed down, struck the earth, sizzled and jumped to one of the tusks of the charging beast. It trumpeted, reared on its hind legs. When it came down, the noise beat Magus' head like hammers.

Smoke drifted from the spot the lightning had seared. The dappled monster seemed unaffected. It waved its sinuous trunk, lowered its head again and came on. The sky erupted red, erupted, erupted again.

Magus stood in the howling wind, his sword blade blown to and fro like a willowy stick.

Move. Move!

He spun, tearing into a run straight back across the bluish turf toward the flower-trees.

He heard the monster right behind. Hans Huygens had babbled of a dappled elephant with eight tusks. Ah God, he'd been right.

Magus shot through the maze of flower trunks and down the slope on the other side. When he screwed his head around in the shrieking wind he saw that the monster had somehow come through the giant flowers too. It bore down on him with amber eyes shining.

His right boot struck air. He fell waist-deep into a hole whose bottom clanged.

He struggled to lift himself from the hole. The aquamarine sward had turned black in the storm. Red lightning seethed back and forth across the sky. The eight-tusk horror lumbered on, tossing its slab head, bellowing with its whipping trunk.

Holding the earth with his hands, Magus kicked against the strange metal sides of the hole. He was exhausted. He knew he could not climb out in time.

XVIII

THE TUSKED HORROR loomed over him. Magus clawed
the aquamarine grass, straightened his arms, lifted
himself half out of the hole. He kicked his legs wide
apart to brace his boots against the hole's metal walls.
Where his right sole struck, the metal buckled.

Thrown off balance, Magus tumbled down into the
hole again. The monster trumpeted. Crumpled at the
bottom of the hole, Magus blinked in confusion.

White pinpoint lights splattered their pattern over his
face.

He discovered the reason the wall of the hole had
given way: the thin metal was formed into a hinged
door measuring about two by two. Pressed inward by
the force of his boot, the door's hatch had come undone.

Something whirred in the dark cavity behind the bent
door. A pierced drum from which the tiny lights shone
rotated with a ratchet-like noise.

The tusked thing roared by above him. Staring up,
Magus saw a lightning-bolt bisect the sky beyond the
hurtling body.

A demon I can see through? There's no such—

Then understanding flooded in. His sword hadn't failed him. The Brothers hadn't bewitched it. The tusk-monster was not real.

The beat of the monster's feet receded, passing away toward the promontory and the ocean. The odd drum rotated deep in the cabinet behind the bent door, *clicka-whirr, clicka-whirr*. Magus remembered the words William Catto had used when he spoke of the house of Easkod.

Image formation.

Image formation.

Magus plunged his hands past the ruined door, clamped them on the revolving drum.

The heat of the drum's surface seared his palms. He held on. He wrenched the drum again. It came loose with a clatter of stripping gears.

He worked the drum out of the cabinet. Now he could see the other equipment in there: a strange hexagonal metal unit with cables of different colors springing from it. The cables disappeared into the dark at the bottom of the compartment. A white dazzle blazed up from an aperture at the hexagon's top. The light-source.

Magus rotated the metal drum in his hands. It was pierced with hundreds of the tiny holes. Transparent lenses were imbedded at intervals around the drum's perimeter.

A faint yellow legend was inscribed on the flat top of the drum. His lips moved, forming the words silently.

"Dimensional Effects Projector. *Projector.*"

He ran a finger down the remainder of the legend. *Model AZ-XR7 Gamma. Corporation of Easkod.*

He gave a ragged laugh. "Magic indeed. Light

magic. Lightmark's light magic. Well, I wonder if it can be exorcised?''

Quickly he bent the thin metal of the door further back. Reaching in, he hit the hexagonal unit with the drum.

He beat on the hexagon until the top began to cave in. One final smashing blow and the surface indented sharply, folding toward the light-source. A hot cracking of glass. A flare and sizzle. A burning smell, a straggle of smoke. The light source blacked out.

Clutching the drum, Magus pulled himself shakily up to the rim of the hole. The sky changed to a shell blue. The flower-trees swayed. The dank forest lay quiet. Distantly the yellow ocean roared.

Magus scowled, searching. He saw no sign that his guess was right—

Yes, there! Directly over his head.

A huge concave patch of glowing gray hit the pale blue sky. His eyes adjusted. He saw the depth relationship correctly. The grayness was some kind of gently shining wall *above* a gap in the sky. He had turned off part of the sky, accounting for the gap and the appearance of the gray surface beyond.

Magus climbed out of the hole. A two-headed serpent slithered from the dank forest. For a moment it watched him with four gemlike eyes. It slid toward him, hissing.

Instead of running from it, he ran toward it. The snake reared. Magus slashed at the double head with the metal drum.

His hand and the drum passed through.

Exactly as he'd expected.

The serpent hissed again, working its wet fangs open

and shut. It retreated toward the flower-trees. Magus headed straight for the dank forest.

He walked into a tree-bole and passed through with no trouble.

He walked through another tree.

Through a clump of ferns.

Through—

His nose smashed something solid.

The wall's visual pattern was the dank forest but its tactile reality was a smooth surface beneath his palms. He felt his way to the left until he came to a place where a semi-cylindrical structure protruded.

He ran his hands over the face of the jutting semi-cylinder, found a stud, pressed it.

A metal door slid upward. A drum-and-hexagon projector three times the size of the one he'd destroyed winked inside the cleverly camouflaged booth. The projector revolved slowly, *clicka-whirr, clicka-whirr*.

Magus seized three of the cables radiating from the hexagon, tugged. A silver plug popped out of a receptacle. Another. The third. He looked back over his shoulder.

Half of the flower-trees were gone. A gray rectangle gaped in the yellow ocean. Laughing, Magus resumed his march around the wall onto which the dimensional forest was projected.

He found the semi-cylindrical booths at regular intervals. One by one he opened them. One by one he pulled all the cables from their projectors.

The sky disappeared section by section.

The ocean blinked off piece by piece.

The eyeball trees went out.

The two-headed serpent reappeared on the promontory. Magus disconnected cables in another booth. The serpent melted away. The turf lost its aquamarine brilliance, revealed as an expanse of long-stranded synthetic carpet.

As he disconnected each one of the machines, the sound level dropped.

The crashing oceans murmured to silence.

Raucous beast cries stilled with a *rrawwwk*.

The wind dwindled.

The last square of lime sky blinked off. Magus stood alone in the center of a vast, circular gray chamber with a high, gently glowing dome.

Marveling, he crossed the floor from side to side. At one point it rose in a gentle incline to form the promontory. The neutral carpeting extended to the promontory's lip, which was supported by a metal scaffolding.

Magus walked on the flat gray surface that had been a foaming stretch of yellow water. Of the original topography of the Hauntplace only the promontory remained as a distinguishable feature. Around the circumference of the lower wall the booths presented smooth, semi-rounded metal exteriors. Even their own camouflage had been projected onto them from booths directly opposite.

In the front of each booth Magus observed apertures of various sizes and shapes. Through these, evidently, the images had been cast. Higher up he noted a series of round grilles. Wind machines? Audio speakers? Possibly both.

He wondered about control of the entire illusion. The Brothers had told him they had never been to the

Hauntplace. Was there a central location elsewhere, one from which the devices could be operated by a single lever or switch? Or had the projectors run constantly for decades, never shut off since the days when human technologists supervised the marvels of Easkod? It was an eerie thought.

Magus climbed the scaffolding. He pulled himself up on the carpet of the promontory and walked down to the nearest booth. Try as he might, he couldn't fathom the principles behind the operation of the drum-and-hexagon.

But he did feel reassured by the knowledge that there was nothing demonic about the projectors. They had been constructed by men. A man could control them. The one Magus was examining even seemed to be portable.

The projector rested on a wheeled base. Extra lengths of colored cable hung on hooks all around it. The cable prongs were color-matched to receptacles in the base. Could the projectors be moved and operated outside the dome? Worth remembering.

Magus let out a long, weary sigh. The ordeal had left him dirty, stinking. But he was alive. And obliged to put the marvels of the Hauntplace out of his mind in favor of more pressing concerns.

Where was Maya? What had become of Catto? He'd answer neither question until he found a way out.

Accordingly, he began to work his way around the wall again. He completed one circuit without discovering a single break in the smooth grayness. A thought struck him.

He wedged into one of the booths. He rolled the

drum-and-hexagon as far to one side as it would go. He groped along the booth's rear wall. His hands brushed a horizontal bar.

Levering it down, he threw his weight forward. The wall opened outward.

A silent corridor curved around away to left and right, following the outer perimeter of the Hauntplace. The floor was smooth, polished, faintly springy under his foot. The walls gave off the same soft glow as inside the dome; not inordinately bright but fully light enough for good visibility. Magus went to the left.

Shortly he reached a junction. A round corridor branched away on his right at a direct right angle. Set into the wall on his left was a small metal plaque engraved with the words CENTER FOR AUDIOVISUAL DEMONSTRATION.

Magus had no notion of what a Center for Audiovisual Demonstration might be. He turned down the branch corridor.

Soon he came to a double door set in the left wall. He touched the hemispherical bulge and the door opened with a mechanical hiss.

Darkness out there. Darkness, and cool wind on his face. He stepped onto a low porch. He walked down three steps. The door shut, cutting off the pale gray light.

Magus felt very much alone as he crossed a narrow avenue into one of the wasted little parts. Easkod City lay still in a sighing wind.

His belly tightened as he set off across the park, moving fast but cautiously.

Find Catto. Find Maya. Those were his tasks now. But where were the Brothers hiding?

XIX

MAGUS CROSSED the park into the deeper shadows beneath one of the overhead pipe runs. A slow thudding drifted on the night air.

The footpads of beasts. Coming at a slow walk up the avenue that ended at the triangular park.

Magus slid into hiding behind one of the silver piers supporting the pipes. Three Brothers mounted on fork-tailed beasts rode out of the avenue's gloom. They were followed by three more.

There was something loathsome in the snakish suppleness of the animals' long necks. Their scaled hides shone damp from internal secretions. The riders crossed the park. They stopped before the door Magus had left only moments earlier.

The Brothers climbed down. The beasts sniffed the earth of the little park. One Brother pulled something from the waist of his kilt and let it ripple out white in the wind.

A scrap of cloth? Why? The answer came momentarily.

The Brother wrapped the cloth around and around his own head. A companion stepped up behind him to adjust it. Then red hands guided the blind Brother up the porch to the doors. The five remaining Brothers faced away from the dome. They covered their eyes with their claw hands. The Brother at the door touched the other bulge. The door hissed open. The Brother walked hesitantly inside.

Gray light flooded the park, then vanished as the door shut again. From the Brothers waiting, a soft *scree-scree* sighed out.

All at once Magus understood.

Plume himself had never entered the Hauntplace. But someone had to fetch the victims back and forth. Magus wondered how the Brother inside was supposed to find the one he sought. Was he permitted to unbind his eyes? Or must he stumble in the Hauntplace until he chanced on the victim?

Victim.

Magus seized on the word. The Brothers had come for him. Therefore Catto would be delivered next. Therefore he had to find Catto and help him if he could.

Cautiously, Magus moved from behind the pier. To reach the mouth of the avenue beyond the park he had to cross a moon-washed stretch. He bent low, took a look to make sure the Brothers on the porch still had their eyes covered. Then he ran.

He dashed straight past the corner of the park toward the shadowed avenue. He'd gone halfway across the open stretch when the beasts somehow sensed his motion. Up came ropy necks. Heads bent back along flanks. Dumb eyes in slab heads searched and searched. The beasts began to stir and stamp.

Still Magus had a quarter of the way to go before he reached cover. One of the beasts grew more restive, lurched against its neighbor. The bumped beast arched its head over and down to bite the first beast's neck.

The other beasts swung their heads, snorting. Hoof-pads struck earth. One Brother took his claws from his bulging eyes. Magus dove for the gloom at the base of a building on the avenue.

Safe for the moment, he covered his mouth and breathed hard. The Brothers were talking to one another. Their *scree-scree* became agitated.

The commotion among the stamping beasts distracted the Brothers enough to give Magus the opportunity to slip down the avenue in the dark. When he could no longer hear the clamor at the dome he slowed his pace and studied his surroundings.

On his left a triangular building showed its silver sides to the sky. They dazzled like mirrors, reflecting the stars. Just past this structure a wider avenue intersected this one at an angle of ninety degrees.

He darted to the corner of the triangular building. He peered along the broader avenue. He recognized it. Two squares to his right stood the parabolic fountain.

He thought he detected signs of movement down there. He crossed the narrower avenue in the direction of the fountain. He stayed close to the base of the next building as he moved along, drawn sword against his side.

His mouth tasted of bitter saliva. He realized how exhausted he was. His body ached from the top of his head to the bones of his feet. For one brief instant he wished he were back on Pastora, torches flaring, crowd gaping as he materialized little green fireballs on the tips of his fingers. Honest or not, it suddenly seemed a most attractive life.

Even pursuit by meccanodogs seemed vaguely nostalgic as he huddled under the metal sweep of a building a block from the fountain. Several beasts were tethered there. Magus saw Catto. The tall man stamped back and forth while four Brothers kept watch, short spears ready.

Magus' legs were growing stiff in the night's cold. He was sleepy. He dug his nails into his palms. It helped only a little. He still felt weary and insignificant in the alien loneliness of this dead city.

He thought of Maya. He was glad she wasn't here to see him hesitate.

Fatigue dulled his mind. Time was slipping away. The Brothers from the dome would return soon, crying that the wizard had disappeared. A search, a pursuit—

Magus shook his head hard.

Concentrate on Catto. Free Catto.

The question remained—how?

The odds were bad: four Brothers against his sword and Catto's fists. He presumed Catto's blaster had been seized and destroyed. He crept forward to a corner of the building nearest the fountain. A good distance still remained between this hiding place and the spot where Catto stood with head tilted up at the stars. His posture suggested tension, anxiety.

Visually Magus measured the distance to the fountain. If he simply charged at the Brothers, they'd see him long before he could strike.

How to distract them? He ransacked his mind like a pack of marketplace tricks.

Tricks?

The deadening fatigue washed away. He was tempted to laugh.

He pulled up his tunic. He dug into the coarse-cloth belt he'd wrapped around his middle when he left the skysled. His fingers probed a small pocket, drew out two of the precious packets of greenish powder.

His hands shook a little as he slipped his sword under one arm to free both hands.

He ripped the packet seal. He poured the first batch of powder into his left hand. Damned if these scaly horrors would kill him. He was Magus Blacklaw. He'd outwitted the best in his day. All it took was the audacity of the unexpected. . . .

He shifted the remaining packet to his teeth, held it thus while he ripped it open with his free hand. He tilted his head. Greenish powder dribbled down into his right hand. A packet's worth in each.

For performances in the marketplace he used a pinch of the pressure-sensitive powder in the V of skin between each two fingers. When he squeezed the fingers together the powder ignited. He could then quickly juggle the fireball to his fingertips.

Tonight a much more spectacular performance! Magus' bearded face took on some of its old glee. He closed both his fists tight.

He felt the heat begin to surge. Trickles of green light bled through the translucence of his hands. He opened his hands and the fireballs bloomed, big as a man's head.

Magus could juggle little balls of the liquid green light for quite some time; the heat was less concentrated. Burning in two such large globes, it seared. He hauled back his right arm, threw the fireball far out in the avenue. Then he hurled the other after the first.

The fireballs lit the avenue from side to side. The

Brothers at the fountain screamed *scree*, turning toward the whirling balls as they dropped, trailing green sparks. Catto was alert. The tethered beasts trumpeted, broke their pickets, lashed their forked tails.

While the four Brothers gaped at the fireballs, Magus ran toward the fountain unobserved. Catto saw him suddenly. A wild grin shone beneath his scraggly red moustaches.

The fireballs hit the pavement and splattered, much of their light spent. A Brother turned, saw Magus coming, struck his comrades with the butt of his spear to draw their attention. But he was nearly on them now. He let out a savage yell for whatever demoralizing effect it might have.

It had considerable. The Brothers huddled into a tight, defensive group. Catto leaped on them from behind.

Catto throttled one of the creatures as Magus ran another through the throat. The gored Brother pitched over.

The one Catto throttled batted at his attacker's head with the butt of his spear. A blow connected. Catto reeled and hit the fountain. He went down awkwardly on his rump.

The strangled Brother spun and ran at Catto with the head of his spear aimed at Catto's bowels. Catto tried to hitch himself out of the way. He wasn't going to be fast enough.

Magus leaped, stretching his sword-arm until the muscle in his shoulder throbbed. The spear flashed at Catto's belly as Magus slashed in from the right. Just as the spear struck, Magus' sword slid in under the running Brother's chin. The black-pupil eyes bulged as the Brother impaled himself.

The spear missed Catto, drew sparks as it glanced off the fountain. Magus absorbed the terrific impact of the impalement. He wrenched so hard he nearly broke his wrist. But he freed his sword. The Brother dropped.

Catto scrambled up. "That's a debt I owe, wizard. I'll—'ware behind you!'"

Whirling, Magus fended the third Brother off. Spear hammered down on sword hilt. Magus heaved upward, threw the Brother off balance. His blade ripped the creature's belly open.

The Brother doubled. His *scree* climbed the scale as he died.

Meantime Catto snatched up a fallen spear. He downed the fourth Brother with three fast strokes.

He raised his head. He pointed up the avenue in the direction of the tallest tower.

"They're riding back. I can hear their beasts."

So did Magus. A low hammering came from the direction of the Hauntplace. He raced over to the Brother Catto had speared.

"This one's still living. Let's take him."

Surprised, Catto said nothing. Magus lifted the Brother onto his shoulder. The chitinous hide and all the alien organs it surrounded proved surprisingly light.

Catto suggested taking sanctuary in the thick shadows on the avenue's far side. They left the fountain at a run, Catto in the lead with a spear flashing in his fist, Magus pelting along behind.

The fireballs sputtered out. The two men plunged down a silver-walled side street as the first Brothers rode out of the avenue that led to the Hauntplace. By the time the Brothers reached the fountain, Magus and Catto were well away.

Catto guided them left, down a narrower street that

paralleled the avenue of the fountain. They went six squares, stopped to rest. Magus flung the Brother against the wall.

The creature uttered feeble cries. Magus went to his knees. His gray-splashed hair was unkempt. His eyes were bloodshot and furious. Catto didn't fail to notice.

"I thought they might have haunted the fight out of you, wizard. I was in error."

Magus waved to indicate the faraway Hauntplace. "Illusion. Mummery." A quick gasp of air. "Tell you . . . about it later." He prodded the Brother. "Do you hear me?"

The Brother's huge black pupils glared his fear. "Hear you. Yes, yes."

"There is a woman, a girl with long hair like this." Magus pantomimed, saw recognition in the Brother's eyes. "Your people have her. She's one of us. I want her back."

No response.

Magus grabbed Catto's spear, touched the head to the Brother's scaly breastbone.

"Tell me where she is or I'll kill you. Do you understand me? You tell me or I'll kill you."

The creature bobbed his head frantically. His body ran with the ooze of his wounds.

The Brother's claw waved in the air in the direction of the tallest tower.

"Behind the great spire we camp. She is there."

"She's there *now?* She's alive?"

"Alive a little time ago, yes, yes. I do not know for certain now. I saw her last before you went to the Hauntplace. You are the magic, the devil." The creature thrashed his hands in the dirt at the foot of the silver wall. His voice became a wail. "You came from the Hauntplace alive!"

"Because my magic is stronger than Brother Plume's. The girl—"

"She was there behind the spire before you went to the Hauntplace—"

Suddenly the creature convulsed with pain. Magus very nearly felt sorry for him.

"I would only tell rightness to the wizard. No falseness, only rightness. You have lived out the Hauntplace. Do not harm me. I have told you the rightness about her."

Magus hesitated. Then, shrugging, he started to release his fingers from the shaft of the spear so he could pass it back to Catto.

Catto reached down for the shaft. With one push-and-twist he crunched the spear through the Brother's chitinous breastbone. Magus' fingers were still curled around it.

The creature stiffened, the horror of betrayal in his distended eyes. Catto released his grip. So did Magus. The spear drooped only a little. The Brother fell over. With a last feeble *scree*.

The tip of the spear protruded through red back scales.

Nauseated, Magus wiped his hands on his breeches. "He told me what I wanted. Why did you kill him?"

William Catto's smile was cruel. "Because I wanted to kill him. I think that's sufficient explanation."

Magus knew a blinding moment of anger and scorn. He stifled it.

He glanced up. The sky seemed a bit lighter. The streets were still. What had happened to their pursuit?

Magus pointed off toward the highest tower.

"The camp's that way. I'm going to find my daughter."

Catto said nothing, fell in step beside him. Shadow among shadows, they moved silently on through the city.

XX

THE WIND FELL. The moon of Lightmark set. A hint of rich purple melted into the blackness of the sky's starred arch. Catto quickened the pace.

"It'll be light in an hour or two."

Magus gave a tight nod. Imagination bedeviled him with scenes of Maya being butchered by the Brothers, or subjected to their curiosity and cruelty in obscene ways. He heard a noise. So did Catto. They stopped.

A subdued roar echoed from the quarter of the city away to the left. They reached a corner. Magus peered down the cross street leading back to the avenue of the fountain. He drew a sharp breath.

On another street a few squares beyond the avenue of the fountain, ranks of mounted Brothers were passing. They stood out dimly against the backdrop of a silver sphere on supporting pylons. The Brothers rode four abreast, appearing and disappearing like a procession behind a proscenium. Some held guttering torches.

Magus counted twenty-five of the creatures. Another twenty-five. Fifty more and still there was no end to them. Their spears shimmered by the light of the occasional torches.

The Brothers were riding on a roadway parallel to the one where Magus and Catto hid. They were riding into the city, toward the central spire.

"Our problem's just worsened," Magus said.

"Aye," Catto agreed. "Perhaps the tall one— what's his name—Plume? Perhaps he sent for reinforcements. After all," he added with small humor, you've cut a wide swathe as a wizard tonight."

"Wherever they came from, the plain or right here in the city, they'll make it harder to find Maya and get her out. Let's keep moving. There may be more of them on the way." He remembered the words of the dying Brother after the first attack. "How many Brothers on Lightmark?" Magus had asked.

"As the pieces of the land." Bits of shale had trickled out of the scaly palm. "As the pieces of the land."

Magus pushed himself now, moving at a near run. Catto kept up.

Before long they'd worked their way to the place where the avenue ended. Opposite was a spacious park with a circular road running around its perimeter. This park, Magus saw thankfully, contained a good deal of the blue-leafed vegetation. Not quite tree-size yet larger than shrubs, the blue plants might provide needed cover.

Magus reasoned that the camp of the Brothers must be located out of sight behind the spire. He heard a faint *scree* blown on the wind. Otherwise the darkness around the spire's base revealed nothing. The spire rose in lonely splendor, so high Magus' neck ached when he tried to see all the way to the top. Halfway up, the immense yellow letters stood out at the end of silver rods.

COPORATION OF EASKOD.

Catto breathed a little harder, like a man seeing a woman he desired.

"Wherever the reinforcements went," Magus said as they moved toward the park, "it wasn't here."

Catto grunted. The roar of the passage of the host of Brothers had died out. The two men reached the park and darted through a clump of blue foliage. Magus' cheek brushed a branch. The blue leaves crumbled on contact. Blue dust drifted down.

Death and decay, Magus thought, *death and decay.* The isolation, the alien silence of Easkod City gripped him again. He fought panic.

As they neared the front of the spire Catto stopped again. He stared at the sculptured canopy flaring out from the tower at a height of three stories. A trio of graceful ramps led from the park up to silver doors a story above. Catto's breath was heavy.

"I've waited a long time to get to this spot." He fixed Magus with a strange unsettling glance. "I suppose I can go with you a bit further and help you find your girl. I suppose I do owe you that much." Something in his voice suggested that he had some doubt.

They crept on around the base of the tower. Magus raised his arm to hold Catto back.

"I see the camp. Here, come up a little more. But quietly."

Catto slid up beside him. Both men crouched, watching.

In the continuance of the park at the back of the spire, Brothers were climbing onto their beasts. A dozen mounted up and rode off. Half a dozen more followed as the first group clattered out of sight.

A last batch of stragglers mounted. Several horns sounded from far away. And again.

Torches of gnarled wood were planted in a bare space among the blue shrubs. In the center of this open space, a crude shelter had been constructed of several brown-furred cloaks thrown over a framework of spears. Two Brothers on the ground in front of the shelter were arguing with the last of the stragglers.

The rider dug bony heels into his beast's flanks. "Remain! Plume summons. He was called a host because the alien wizard is free in holy Easkod working his deviltry. Plume councils with the host in the great park this moment. Some must wait, some must watch the wizard's woman-thing."

Angry, one of the Brothers in front of the shelter stamped the butt of his spear in the dirt. "We have a privilege of riding to war. We are no less than you. We say—"

"Plume has ordered two watchers. You are chosen. Wait and keep clear eyes."

The Brother on beast-back spoke loudly, with unmistakable command. The slit mouths of the others shut as the rider kicked his mount and hammered away. The lashing forked tail disappeared in a welter of dust and pulverized blue leaves.

The dust settled. The torches popped, flared into tatters of flame. The angry Brother squatted again, growling at his more phlegmatic companion.

"Not good," Catto breathed. "No doubt that bastard Plume'll use his reinforcements to search the city. Goddamn them for smashing the hand blaster."

"Go if you want! Go on into the tower and play with your dead toys if that's all that concerns you."

Catto scowled. "Have I said a word about leaving? When the time comes, you'll know. Meanwhile"—faint contempt in his voice—"what do you suggest we do?"

Magus spent some seconds studying the terrain. If they circled wide to their right through the concealment of the blue shrubs, then came up behind the shelter and the guards, surprise might be on their side. It was a better strategy than a frontal attack. Mounted Brothers might still be within hailing distance.

Magus dug under his tunic. He pulled out several silks he'd salvaged from the skysled. Catto frowned at the yellow and white and pale blue frothing in Magus' clenched fist.

"Have you lost your sanity? What good are common silks?"

"Uncommon silks." Magus shoved the yellow one at Catto. "Pull it. Try to tear it. They're woven with metallic filaments. Strong enough to support three men my size. I've bound a thousand fools who thought they could rip free, and won a ha'credit every time. We'll take the silks . . ."

Magus whispered on for the better part of a minute.

At the end Catto gave a grudging nod. He and Magus glided into the dark to their right. They began working their way around behind the shelter.

Catto blundered into a shrub. He cursed softly as an audible rain of pulverizing leaves pattered down. Magus froze where he was, squinting.

One of the Brothers stood up. He took a few paces, listening. In the distance horns bleated again. A man-voiced *scree! scree! scree!* came floating among the towers.

Plume exhorting his host? And they responding, savagely, with cries of rage against the desecrators? Whatever was transpiring at the rendezvous point, it served to distract the guard. The creature turned back and fell to grumbling over his lot.

Magus moved forward again. Catto followed. A tiny stone had worked its way into Magus' left boot. It cut his flesh. A small thing, a cursed distraction; it made every step more and more painful.

Finally he and Catto worked themselves into position behind the shelter. Magus quieted the rattle of his sword-sheath. He lifted his left hand up near his right, stretched the pale blue silk between, snapped it taut.

He heard nothing from inside the shelter.

Oh, God if only Maya would speak! Breathe in terror, even, so he might know—

Perhaps she could make no sound. Perhaps she'd been mutilated, subjected to vile—

Magus wiped his eyes on his sleeve to clear them of sudden sweat. Chewing his lower lip, Catto watched him closely. Magus' left leg throbbed from the steady pain of the rock in his boot. He felt dizzy. He wanted to scream Maya's name. He fought the urge, crossed his wrists, nodded to Catto, slunk forward.

Catto slipped around the left side of the shelter. Magus took the right. They emerged into the flicker of the torches. Magus shot his hands forward, whipped the sky blue silk down over the head of the squatting Brother.

A little slower, Catto snapped his silk into place just as his creature saw Magus from the corner of one bulging eye. A screaming *scree* came from the slit mouth.

Magus uncrossed his wrists. The filament silk cut

into the Brother's throat. The creature yelped, thrashed, tried to rise. Magus jammed a knee into the scaled back, pulled hard with both hands.

Catto's luck was not as good. His creature managed to twist, drive his spear at Catto's left thigh. Catto had to loosen his hold to jump out of the way.

The momentum of the creature's lunge carried him off balance. Catto snatched the ends of the silk, gave a sudden jerk that pulled the creature's head up hard. Catto thrust his knee under the Brother's bony jaw. He wrapped the creature's head tight in the silk, caught both ends in one hand, lifted the Brother's head and smashed it down on his knee.

Lift, smash. Lift, smash. Lift, smash. The chitinous line of chin softened. The black-pupiled eyes bulged out and out. Ooze leaked from the slit mouth.

Panting, Magus was pulling his Brother from side to side. The creature sliced the air with his spear, trying to thrust behind him. Magus dodged one way, then the other. A stink of excitement leaked from the creature's hide as it caught hold of Magus' left leg and dug in its claws.

The sudden pain robbed Magus of strength. He went down, his hands ripping away from the ends of the blue silk wound around the Brother's throat.

A commotion. Voices in the shelter. The flapping of furred cloaks thrown aside. Slamming down hard on his back, Magus saw nothing of it.

The Brother stepped on his throat and pinned him. The creature thrust the spear at Magus' face. Magus tried to wrench aside.

A hand, a black ring blazing, gripping the spear. Turning it violently.

The creature cried *scree*. Magus blinked through the

dust, saw a glare of gold eyes, thought he was going mad. The Brother's own spear was turned back and plunged into his scaled belly.

Then a boot kicked the Brother's kilted loins. The creature staggered back to fall, died with the spear still upright in its middle.

"Father!"

Maya lunged against him, flung her arms around his neck. Her face was a blur of bruised flesh, tangled hair, violet eyes. He felt his own tears of joy as he held her close.

"Maya. Ah girl, girl." He thrust her away gently, studied her face. "They've hurt you. Marks all over your cheeks, your forehead." His mouth wrenched as he touched her hair.

She could hardly speak coherently, crying again: "It's not so bad, Father, not so bad—"

Suddenly Magus' eyes focused on the man standing behind them. The man with yellow-white hair and wild gold eyes. The man with a black ring on the last finger of his right hand and a wounded arm bound with what appeared to be a piece of Maya's underslip.

Robin Dragonard had been inside the shelter. Robin had slain the Brother attacking Magus.

Robin said, "I stayed with Philosopher Lantzman as long as I could stomach him. Then I came on here alone, to find her."

Robin's quite understatement spoke more of his love for the girl than ever a long speech would have done. After a minute he went on:

"I hadn't gotten far into the city when the Brothers discovered me. I fought but there were too many. They brought me here. They put me inside with Maya. I would have tried to escpae but Maya wanted to wait. She hoped you'd come. Captured or otherwise.'' Robin glanced at Catto, who studied him with cynical amusement. "I may have been a damn fool but I take back nothing. Not how I feel about Maya most of all.''

Slowly Magus nodded. All he could say was, "Good, Robin. Good.''

In the distance the horns blared. A drumming began off among the towers.

Catto's eyes went huge. "They're coming back. Everybody up! Up and run for it!''

XXI

THE FOUR OF THEM stayed in the park only long enough to drag the two dead Brothers into the shrubs behind the shelter. Magus took the spear Robin had used and slashed at the branches. As the blue leaves fell, a powdery silt built up on the corpses.

Coughing, Magus finally stepped back. He was satisfied. In the uncertain light of the approaching dawn, the shapes of the slain Brothers could barely be detected beneath the leaf flakes. He hoped that when the Brothers came back, they would think that his magic powers had vanished both guards and guarded. Perhaps it would help delay pursuit.

The pound of beast hooves grew louder.

They circled the tower, raced across the front park and plunged down one of the avenues leading away to the edge of the city. Magus' chest ached. His head throbbed. The accumulated fatigue and tension of the long night were taking toll.

But Maya was as one reborn. She ran with her face lifted to the wind, her russet hair streaming. The wash of light from the stars made her eyes shine like medallions as she turned to smile at Robin beside her. Robin's gold eyes gave her back the smile. She caught his hand.

Well, Magus thought, *at least this much has come out right. Though it's still a long way to—*

To where? They were fleeing without plan or purpose.

They crossed another intersecting avenue. Magus realized that he must decide what to do next. They couldn't run endlessly around and around the silver city a hand's width ahead of Brother Plume and his host. But he was too exhausted to think clearly.

Maya's cry brought him spinning around.

She'd caught her bare foot in a crack between the paving stones. She tumbled, hitting her head.

Robin and Catto skidded to a stop. The gold-eyed man dropped to his knees beside her. "I thought she saw the broken place," Robin breathed.

Magus rubbed her wrists and pinched her cheek. She blinked and sat up.

"Just got the breath knocked out of you," Magus said.

"We've got to go on," Maya said, struggling to rise. "They'll—"

William Catto hefted his spear. "The girl's right. Two of these and one spear are all we have left for fighting."

The decision came to Magus then. He felt as though he'd sipped a draught of cool wine. His pulse slowed down. His mind unscrambled itself from the nightmare of constant motion, attack, flight. He rose and glanced at the paling stars.

"We're leaving," he said. "Maya, Robin—we're leaving. We'll go straight out of the city to the skysled."

"So hastily?" Catto asked. "What about your plans?"

"Plans?"

"To loot devices from the buildings? Carry them back to Pastora and use them to build your fortune?"

Magus glanced at his daughter. She was unsteady on her feet. Resolve cut into him, met his dream of riches and shattered it with a suddenness that left him empty and tired again. He replied: "There's a time when wisdom speaks a little louder than greed."

"I'm to stay behind, is that it?"

Magus shrugged. "The choice is yours. You're the one who stowed away."

With the tip of his spear the tall man drew a cross in the dust. He obliterated it with a quick motion, began to trace out a letter.

Catto's thick red brows concealed his eyes as he angled his head lower, watched his own hand trace another letter and another.

EAS

Catto sniffed. He studied the stars. He listened to the wind. His red-haired hand kept moving.

EASKO

Magus listened too. The *scree-scree* cries of the Brothers below down the wind from the direction of the central spire. Walls of buildings began to reflect glow of coming day. Catto finished the name in the dust.

EASKOD

Muttering something that sounded like an obscenity, he struck the dust with the spear. The name was gone.

"One thing I don't understand. What happens when you reach Pastora."

Magus managed a smile. Some of his old dash and bravado returned. He felt confident, in charge of things once again. "Why, nothing. I've performed my mission. I've exorcised the demons of Lightmark. I'll simply tell the High Governors that at first I thought the Brothers were supernatural, thus accounting for my early reports. Then I discovered otherwise. I'll have fulfilled the letter of the contract the Governors forced on me and I'll be free." He caught Maya's elbow. "Stand up, girl."

Catto pointed to the wafer tied to Magus' throat. "Why don't you tell the Governors now?"

"First things first. It can wait until we're safely home."

"And then you intend to say there are no spirits, no devils, no enchantments here?"

"Only machines," said Magus. "Isn't that essentially the message you gave me when we met? It took a while for me to be convinced. You see, Catto, down deep I believed in the demons at first. So in a sense you can say I truly have exorcised them. From within myself."

"Talk that way on Pastora and no one will believe you."

"I think they will for two reasons: I'll have witnesses. And the Governors trapped me into coming here because they *want* Lightmark to be reachable again. The hour's struck for this place. The demons are all dead and"—Magus shivered in the chill wind. —"it's merely an empty old city full of rather amazing things we've feared for too long. Plus a race of savage mutants too changed to understand that their attitude about Easkod's holiness are wrong. The Brothers may be fearsome, but they can be conquered. It'd be dangerous for you to stay here, Catto. Come back with us."

Catto licked his lips. He raked his hand through his

red hair. A puff of blue leaf dust clouded down over the shoulders of his cloak.

"All right. I'll come."

Robin sucked in an angry breath. Magus stilled him with a look. Catto caught the interplay, laughed unpleasantly.

"I didn't say how far, did I? Only to the edge of the city. I'll lend you what support I can till you're safely onto the plain. I can't go back to Pastora. It took me too long to come this far." He paused and breathed. "Easkod is still mine."

On that question Magus preferred to keep silent. Catto's possessive attitude would be debated by the High Governors, to say the least. But argument now would be pointless, even harmful. He accepted Catto's decision with a nod.

"We'd better start. Can you walk, Maya?"

Before the girl could answer, Catto raised a finger to his mouth. They listened.

In the unnatural stillness no creature-voices cried anywhere.

"Very odd," Catto said. "All that host inside the city and not a sound of it."

"Perhaps Plume's found the dead ones," Magus said. "Perhaps some ritual accounts for the silence."

"I suggest you let me reconnoiter. Check the nearby avenues to see which seems safest. I may pick up some hint of what Plume's up to."

An objection that they couldn't afford the time came instantly to Magus' lips. But Catto moved too fast. He faded into the shadows down the cross street. His spear-hand caught a random bit of light, winked in the shadows, went out.

"We'll probably never see him again," Robin growled.

Magus clucked his tongue. "I believe we will."

Maya shivered. "What a strange man. Such moods. Something's gnawing away down deep inside him. You only see it occasionally, in his eyes or . . ." She gave a little puzzled shake of her head and huddled closer to her father.

"He has all the signs of being a madman," Robin said. "We're well rid of him."

Magus kept his peace, preferring not to fan a new argument.

The sky grew lighter. Magus guessed that full dawn was about an hour away. His right leg had fallen asleep. It tingled with annoying pinpricks. He yawned.

A forced march to the skysled and they'd be safe. The benevolent despotism of Pastora seemed infinitely desirable, and a very long way away.

Robin squatted down to watch. Magus sat. So did Maya. She rested her head against his leg. His eyelids drooped.

He saw a smiling, buxom widow of New Delft unfastening the pins in her hair and beckoning to him, beckoning so warm, so desirable, so rich with life—

"*Wizard!*"

The sibilance of the low cry tore him out of his doze. They all scrambled up. Catto glided out of the dark.

"Well?" Magus snapped.

"I saw nothing. No sign of them. Yet I have a feeling—put it like this: the back of my neck tells me they're moving out there. I don't know. I may be wrong. I suggest we take the avenue of the fountain. We can make better time."

Magus assented with a nod. They started out, four incredibly tiny figures against the massive loom of the towers. Robin breathed loud as a hissing cat.

They reached the avenue. They turned toward the city's perimeter. They moved fast, nearly running. The parabolic fountain appeared ahead. Magus squeezed his daughter's hand.

"We'll make it, girl. Only a bit more now."

There was sudden thunder.

Robin spun to the rear. His gold eyes flickered with fear for an instant. Catto hauled around too. A great obscene oath roared up from his chest.

Magus turned, saw.

Hot tears of frustration sprang into his eyes. *Unmanly!*

Yet they'd been so close. So close . . .

Down the avenue from the central spire the Brothers came riding six abreast. Plume's horny head-spine bobbed in the front rank.

XXII

THEY RAN before the red horde, straight down the avenue toward the fountain. By the time they reached it Magus knew flight was hopeless.

The sound of the feet of the fork-tailed beasts rolled and crashed and echoed between the silver buildings. The *scree* cries of the Brothers were excited, vengeful, victorious.

Magus clambered up on the ledge around the fountain to look back. The creatures were only eight squares behind.

Now seven.

Six.

"You goddamn fool, get down!" Catto bellowed

A huge shudder of tiredness worked over Magus. For a moment he thought he'd faint. All at once the lassitude dropped away. He felt exhilarated. Maya blinked, puzzled because a smile had twisted onto her father's face all at once. His hazel eyes shone with a wild glee.

The riding Brothers were only four squares away.

Three.

"All right, wizard," Catto cried. "The rest of us won't stay to be killed because you've lost your mind."

Magus ignored him. He dug under his tunic, pulled out the last packets of fireball powder. Quickly he tore them. Quickly he emptied all the powder into one hand and squeezed.

"A little diversionary tactic, if you please." There was a laughing madness on him. "When this goes off, run for that street to the left."

"Have you some magical weapons hidden away?" Catto sneered.

"No, but the dead men of Easkod City do. I'm going to stage the finest performance Magus Blacklaw ever gave!"

Sweat streamed down his face. He felt the heat against his constricted palm. He flung his hand high. The green ball burst blindingly above him.

Maya screamed. Magus jumped down from the fountain. Cloak belling out, he looked like some flapping, flying demon silhouetted against the green fire. Robin made the sign against evil eye.

The fireball struck the paving stones. It burst into spitting fragments. Magus shoved Robin and Maya.

"Run!"

He dashed past them, leading the way into the tangle of cross streets. Catto swore and followed.

Magus took a right turning, a left. Behind them the pound of beast-feet slowed a little.

Magus tried to orient himself. It was difficult running at full speed. Clusters of silvery pipe flashed overhead. A wrong corner turned and they were in a cul-de-sac, forced to go back.

"Do you know where you're going?" Catto shouted.

"To the dome," Magus replied.

"Which dome?"

But Magus was already half a square ahead, Robin and Maya right behind.

At the next corner Magus slowed, saw unfamiliar buildings, cried out in rage. Oh, God, he was lost.

No, there it was! Away to his left the dome reflected the feeble stars.

Magus led the way to the little park. They ran up the porch to the silver doors. His shaking hand slid over the door's surface, found the bulge, pressed and with a hiss the door swung away. As Catto and the others clustered behind him he said: "This is their Hauntplace. There are devices inside which—never mind, just follow me." And off he went again, jackboots hammering.

He ran down the corridor to where the bright-metal plaque gleamed. CENTER FOR AUDIOVISUAL DEMONSTRATION. He skidded left into the curving corridor that ran around the perimeter of the dome. He stopped outside an entrance to one of the booths, levered the door open, began pulling and hauling at the wheeled hexagon-and-drum.

"Go around me, Catto. Find another machine like this. Robin, you too. The machines are on wheels. Pull one to the porch."

The projector proved heavier than expected. With difficulty he jockeyed it into the corridor as the other three disappeared from the booth, gone into the dome's interior.

Magus rolled his shoulder against the bulky device. He shoved hard, felt it start to roll. He maneuvered it down to the access corridor, then outward to the doors and onto the porch.

He raced back inside to find Catto just passing the

plaque. Puffing and swearing, Catto moved his projector by himself. Maya and Robin struggled with a third. Magus ran to help them.

"These machines project illusions," he panted as he helped pull the wheeled apparatus into the access corridor. "If I can only—"

"The Brothers are at the head of the avenue," Catto cried from the porch.

Magus left the last unit to Robin and his daughter, joined Catto on the porch. The red-haired man pointed across the park. The sour bile of fear rose to Magus' mouth.

On the narrow street that led to the dome the Brothers rode four abreast. Plume was still at the head, about five squares distant.

Magus helped Robin and Maya roll their projector onto the porch alongside the other two. "Inside, girl. Inside and close the door. Go with her, Robin. You too, Catto."

"The is lunatic," Catto protested. "The surest way to die I've—"

"Will you stop your damned clack and go inside? I will do this thing my way. If it fails, well . . ." He managed a cavalier shrug. The old Magus Blacklaw looked out of his fatigue-darkened eyes. "There'll be only one body here, not four. And you can try running again."

He shoved them back inside and pulled the silver doors shut.

Drumma-drum. Drumma-drum. Magus didn't turn around. The back of his neck crawled. He heard the Brothers riding slowly, *drumma-drum.*

Had they reached the park? He forced himself to be

deliberate in his movements. What if they cast spears at his back? *Don't think of it!*

He lifted his tunic, delved again into the coarse-cloth belt. With great care he wrapped his waist with the scarlet sash stitched silver with arcane symbols.

Then he turned around.

He stepped up between two of the projectors and laid his hands on them as though they were old friends. The wind blew his cloak around his legs. One of the fork-tailed beasts snorted and switched its sinuous neck. Its rider gouged its flank with his scaled heel. The beast quieted.

The Brothers were drawn up on the far side of the park. Fierce, tall, his spiny crest sharp against the lightening sky, Plume urged his beast forward a few paces and there again halted. He rested a short spear against his scaled thigh.

In his best theatrical voice Magus said, "I bid you turn back and bother us no more. I bid you leave Easkod City and never return."

Brother Plume's slit-mouth worked. The expression on his rigid scaled face couldn't change. But his distended white eyes with their black pupils conveyed his hate.

"Desecrator. Desecrator, you."

Magus shook his head. "No. Rightful heir to this magic." He stroked a projector. "These were made by men for use by wizards. I am a wizard. I have walked alive from the Hauntplace."

Out in the host Magus heard the word whispered: *Hauntplace*. The Brothers stirred uneasily.

Plume raised his spear, lashed it down against his beast's hide with a clack. The gesture quieted the ranks.

Magus sensed a new fear in the little park all at once—Plume's overmastering fear that he, leader, might soon have none to lead.

Seizing the mood of the moment, Magus continued in a voice that grew louder and more oratorical: "I have walked from the Hauntplace and brought its magic with me. See, it does me no harm. See, I lay my hands upon it. Do not force me to use this magic against you. If that comes to pass you will surely die." Now Magus spoke not at Plume but beyond him, to his followers. "Do not allow yourselves to be deceived. You have rightly feared the Hauntplace all your lives. Only I, a wizard from out of the sky, can control its magic and shape it to my will. Do not let a frightened leader force you forward to your own destruc—"

"I speak for the Brothers!" Plume interrupted. "They do not speak, desecrator. Only I, Plume, speak!"

"Then speak and tell them to leave Easkod City forever. Else I'll summon the power of this Hauntplace magic and kill you all."

Plume was silent.

Magus wanted to laugh. He'd won. Terrifying them, he'd won. Sweat trickled around his ears into his beard. The wind flapped his cloak loudly, *snaap*.

Abruptly Plume raised his head. The slit-mouth worked.

"Easkod City is ours by right and birth. You are the desecrator. Therefore if you can lay hands on the magic of the Hauntplace, so can we—with no harm."

The high-pitched voice quavered. Magus knew the price Plume must have paid to say what he did: every word ran counter to a lifetime of fear.

The Brothers no longer stirred. Suddenly Plume let out a single wailing *scree*. He flung back his scaled arm and threw the spear straight at the porch.

The ranks of Brothers boiled with cries of anger. Spears flashed, rising—

Plume's spear clanged against the central projector, caromed off. *Ah, wizard, not such a great performance after all.*

Shrieking, Plume signaled his riders forward. Magus dove behind the nearest projector.

He seized a blue plug of eight prongs, jammed it into a matching blue receptacle. A yellow cord, a yellow receptacle—union.

Spears clanged and clattered against the projectors. As he struggled with the cords, Magus wondered whether his last curtain had begun its fall.

XXIII

HE CUT HIS HAND thrusting the final plug into its receptacle. He sucked at the blood as he waited for the *clicka-whirr*, the gleam of light through the piercings of the drum.

No light. No sound.

Magus beat his fist against the hexagon. He crawled to the next projector. A spear slithered between the units, plucked at his cloak.

Blood turned his fingers slippery as he thrust new plugs into matching receptacles. Out of sight, Brother Plume shrilled commands at his followers. Beasts stamped. *Scree* cries crisscrossed one another as orders were passed down the ranks.

With all the cords connected on the second projector, Magus held his breath.

Clicka-whirr. Clicka-whirr.

He banged his knees crawling to the third projector. He got the plugs covered with gore as he fitted them into place. He was conscious of the tremendous roar as the Brothers advanced across the park, conscious of the whiz and whang of spears grazing the sides of the projectors or striking dome above him and sliding down. One hit point first near his foot. It threw off hissing sparks on impact.

As he thrust the last plug home he heard the spurred heels of Brothers clicking on the lower steps of the porch.

All at once the air above changed color. A mammoth orange sun loomed. It fell out of the sky as it had fallen from the sky of the Hauntplace, trailing arms of burning gas. The Brothers moaned their terror.

The phantom sun ate the sky, so real Magus could again imagine its heat on his face. He heard the Brothers calling to one another. Over them came Plume's voice.

"Do not be frightened. Attack him where he hides!"

Magus reached out, seized the projector to his right. The metallic surface was searing. He held fast, hauled himself to his feet.

He stumbled between the projectors out toward the front of the porch. Only a display of absolutely foolhardy courage would turn them. To skulk would undo it all.

The orange sun boiled down to engulf him. In its dazzle he saw the silhouettes of many Brothers, the upthrust of many spears. The orange sun swallowed them all—

And went out.

Magus was alone on the porch. Below him at the porch's edge scores of Brothers crouched. Their slit-mouths worked in silent supplication to whatever gods they still feared. Waiting, shuffling back away from him, they still kept their spears, up ready to kill.

"The magic of the Hauntplace is mighty," Magus shouted. "Do not doubt any longer."

He flung his arms wide, He shut his eyes. He began to rattle off an incantation which sounded sonorous but was in fact gibberish.

Against his own voice he heard Brother Plume's wheedling, snarling, arguing. Plume was trying to force his followers to attack again. Magus kept droning, head thrown back like some mad mystic. What in hell's name had happened to the second projector?

A Brother screamed. Magus snapped his eyes open.

Materializing yonder by the high-soaring pipes, the eight tusked earth-shaker with amber eyes charged straight at the Brothers in the park.

Its dappled flanks heaved. It tossed its snout and trumpeted. Magus detected the sound emanating from all sides of the projector's hexagonal base. It seemed to flow around him like a liquid.

The illusion-beast reared. Its trunk whipped at heaven. When it came down there was thunder.

The Brothers turned and fled.

Somewhere Brother Plume screamed at them to stop. No use. Clank and clank and clank, spears were cast down and forgotten.

The Brothers reached their fork-tailed beasts. They were clubbing each other now, murdering each other in their haste to flee. Magus saw one Brother killed by a spear in his back. The killer trampled the corpse, seized the tether-rope of the waiting beast.

The Brothers choked the avenue for blocks. Of a sudden the press began to ease. The ones in the rear-most ranks were riding out. The rest followed. In moments only a few remained, dead or trampled. Their spears littered the ground like cut grain.

The illusion-monster hurled at the porch, casting a

glaring light on Magus where he stood wiping sweat from his eyes. He began to shudder with shock. He turned back toward the dome doors to call Maya and the others. A horny-crested shape lunged at him along the porch.

Red hands seized the nearest projector, teetered it to the edge of the steps. It crashed down. The image of the tusked monster tilted in the air. The beast seemed to run while lying on its side.

With a *squarrwk* the hexagonal base stopped transmitting sound. Silently the monster worked its huge legs a few more seconds. Then it melted, faded into a spot of light as the glow inside the overturned drum dimmed out. A smell of burning filled the air.

The silhouette took on dimension, solidity. Magus waved in a tired way.

"Go with them, Plume. They've all gone. Gone from the city. Back to the plain. Go with them."

Brother Plume was wounded in the chest. Perhaps it had happened in a fight with one of his reluctant followers. He advanced, his toes clicking. His scarlet fingers were tight around the short spear held horizontally before him.

"Not magic, those. Not magic. Tricks of deviltry. *Tricks!*"

Screaming, Plume lunged.

Magus hauled at the steel at his waist, got it free. Plume's spear struck a shattering blow to the back of his hand. His fingers sprang open. Plume snatched the fallen sword and sailed it into the dark.

Making little hissing noises from his slit-mouth he began to inch his way toward Magus again.

Without hesitation Magus went for the dome doors.

He reached for the knob-like prominence that would open them. Plume's claws flashed down over his head and pulled the spear hard against his throat from behind.

Magus couldn't breathe. Plume pulled the spear harder and harder against his neck. Magus grappled behind him, trying to gain a hold on the scaly body. His hand slipped in the secretion from Plume's wound.

All at once there was emptiness under Magus' left boot. Plume let out a *scree* of rage. Together he and Magus tumbled down the porch steps.

Plume lost his grip on the spear. Its head raked Magus' throat. He hit the overturned projector, rolled away. He tasted the dirt of the park.

Behind him somewhere Plume breathed with a sustained, violent sound. Magus saw a cast-down spear glimmering. He stretched out his right arm. It ached and burned. He groaned, throwing himself forward. He caught the spear and rolled over on his back as Brother Plume came staggering, his own spear angled down at Magus' belly.

With a final unthinking effort Magus shoved upward. Plume's shaft grazed his chest. The leader of the band of Brothers impaled himself on the shaft that Magus had waiting.

Plume fell.

After a minute Magus crawled away, rose painfully. He tottered back to the tall Brother. Plume's huge black-pupiled eyes fastened on him, uncomprehending.

Around the spear shaft buried in Plume's middle stinking fluid bubbled. It drained down his flank to stain his kilt. Magus felt dizzy. His head rang like a gong.

"Plume? If you were ever human, you . . . never lost all of it. It was a brave thing, staying when the rest ran away." Magus licked his lips. "Brave. Plume? It was brave. Do you know what that means? Do you know what I'm saying to you?"

Brother Plume gave a last meaningless *scree*. He died.

Shaking his head, Magus stumbled back up to the porch. He could hardly see. He reached for the knob device. It shot away from him into space that distorted. Magus tried to grope across the widening gulf of dark and tumbled into it.

When he awoke the stars over Lightmark were gone. It was morning.

He saw the carnage: Plume's ghastly corpse; the bodies of dead Brothers; a litter of discarded spears; the overturned projectors. Dull pain tortured his body. William Catto crouched in front of him, watching.

Magus started up. "Maya—"

"I'm here."

She blurred into the corner of his vision, coming down from the porch. She looked weary. So did Robin right behind her. All of them were filthy, disheveled, their faces covered by bruises and small wounds.

Magus licked dust away from the corners of his mouth. He started to rise. Catto helped him. There was a curious smile on Catto's face.

"Whatever you did, wizard, it must have been a magnificent performance. I've searched and scouted for blocks around. There's not a sign of a Brother left. Did you kill the big one? Their leader?''

"Yes," Magus said, not proud of it.

"Now we can leave this slaughterhouse," Robin said.

Catto's red eyebrows pinched together. "Why hurry now? We're safe."

"We'll never be safe until we're back on Pastora," Maya said.

"Of course you're safe," Catto insisted. "I tell you the Brothers are gone. You understand, don't you, wizard? Now you can take the time to collect your scientific apparatus. Pack up a whole load of them. You can do it in an hour or two. I'll show you. Come." He tugged at Magus' arm. "Let's go to the central spire. We'll find what you want there, wizard."

Maya stepped between Catto and her father. Her violet eyes shone in the new sunlight.

"It isn't necessary," she said. "What if the Brothers should come back? Nothing is worth another night like the one we went through. Nothing."

Magus thrust her aside. His mind wasn't quite functioning. Something warned him that there was a trap in Catto's persuasion, a pitfall which ought to be readily apparent but was not. The old greed swept over him. He remembered long, lonely roads on Pastora. He remembered his vow to make certain Maya never lived that kind of life again.

"All right, Catto. We'll stay long enough to collect our deserved rewards. A few magical devices to bemuse and bedazzle the poor clods in the market towns. We'll be rich when we get home!"

"Listen to Maya," Robin Dragonard begged him. "Why risk it?"

"Because I *say* we'll risk it, damn you, boy! You may not appreciate the niceties of an empty purse, but I've had a bellyful of being poor. Catto said the Brothers have gone. It's evident he's right. Where's the harm? Take Maya back to the skysled if you want. Your option. I won't run with you."

He shoved past Robin to follow Catto, who was already loping across the park in his peculiar quick stride.

Reluctantly Maya and Robin fell in behind. They turned into the avenue of the fountain and proceeded toward the central spire, bright silver in the full light of day.

Once more a wind sang among the towers. But the earth no longer trembled with the passage of beasts. The Brothers had truly gone. Magus suspected that without Plume, they might never ride into Easkod City again.

He found himself whistling off key as he swung along beside William Catto. The red-moustached man had the only weapon left to them now, a single spear. Magus had clean forgotten about retrieving his sword. He supposed it didn't matter.

"'Ware ahead!" Robin said.

William Catto planted his boots on the paving stones. "I'll be damned ten times over."

The spire's sculptured canopy caught sun, flared with highlights. Below it two men stood near the three curving ramps that led up to silver doors.

One wore yellow boots.

The other had gray hair.

Philosopher Arko Lantzman and his bravo.

Both had their daggers drawn.

XXIV

WILLIAM CATTO STARED up the avenue at the figures beneath the sweeping canopy. His thumb moved back and forth on the shaft of the spear he held in his right hand. The ball of the thumb pressed harder. The thumb moved back and forth faster.

"Only two of them," he said finally. "Well, why put it off?" His smile was not pleasant.

Catto swung into his peculiar long stride, heading straight toward the park in front of the great spire. Magus hesitated. He felt uneasy again.

His daughter's violet eyes seemed to plead: *Back to the skysled*. His glance slid away. Greed tugged. He started walking.

As Magus followed Catto up the avenue, he noticed a subtle change in the man's posture. Catto had thrown off his weariness. His body angled forward slightly, as though he were eager for an encounter with the two waiting by the ramps. Magus heard Robin and Maya coming along now. Robin's boots hit hard on the pavement. Magus didn't look back. He wished he had a weapon.

They crossed the park of stunted shrubs. Catto set bluish clouds of leaves to whirling and falling as he passed. Magus caught up with him just as he reached the foot of the ramp where Lantzman and his bravo waited.

The bravo's dagger caught sun as his nervous hand played with it. The man's eyes slid across Magus' face and away. Resentful. Fearful. Probably recalling how the thug with the scarred chin had died.

Philosopher Lantzman looked runtier, more exhausted than ever. His skin and clothes were filthy. In his beard a morsel of food glistened. He and Catto eyed each other.

"I thought you'd come here," Lantzman said. "That is, if you survived the attack by the Brothers. I gather the wizard had something to do with sending the creatures back to the plain? Not exactly the outcome you wanted, is it, Catto? I was sure you would survive the attack however."

"You're talking nonsense," Catto replied.

"Is he?"

Magus turned, startled. Robin strode to a point midway between the two men. But he spoke to Lantzman: "There's a meaning in what you just said, isn't there? A meaning we were meant to catch."

"You're perceptive, Dragonard," Lantzman answered. "I don't mind telling you that, even though you did walk out on us because of the girl. Yes, there is a meaning. My bodyguard and I came into the city just before dawn. We kept to the side streets. From a distance we saw the Brothers assembling for what I gathered was a concerted attack on someone or something. Just as we were passing one of the cross-avenues back there we heard a commotion. We hid. We saw something most interesting. Most revealing."

Catto's thumb worked fast again up and down the spear shaft. Philosopher Lantzman began to walk in a small circle. His overfed belly thrust out with a trace of arrogance, as though he knew he'd suddenly seized control of the little group. He picked at his beard. He stared off into the sky, amused, musing. At last he continued:

"What we saw begins to take on significance now, don't you see? For here's William Catto right with you. Defender of your safety, eh? He's the only one who has a weapon left so he must have fought alongside you. There was a fight, yes? We certainly heard the sounds of it. Then the Brothers rode away howling. But earlier, when my companion and I hid, observed, we saw a most curious sight. . . ."

"That's enough!" Catto cried, starting forward.

The yellow-booted bravo whipped his knife hand up across his chest. Lantzman shifted his dagger into striking position too. Catto stopped, checked by the two knives ranged against his spear.

Arko Lantzman giggled. "I don't wonder you're not anxious to have me talk."

"Speak out plain, Philosopher," Magus said. "What did you see?"

Lantzman licked his lips. "This man Catto whispering with three Brothers."

"Lies!" Catto began.

"Go on," said Magus.

"One Brother slipped off quickly in the direction of the spire, as though carrying a message. Catto remained until the other two left. Then he went his own way. It was almost as though he'd brought the Brothers certain information—"

The hate that rose in Magus' throat nearly choked him. He whipped Catto around by the shoulder.

Instinctively Catto raised his spear. Maya let out a little cry. Robin shifted forward half a step.

"The Brothers wouldn't have killed you at the dome, would they, Catto?" Magus snarled.

"You're making the assumptions, not I."

"Yes, and my assumption is this: when you left us saying you were going to reconnoiter you searched until you found a scouting party of Brothers. You told them where we were. Then you came back. You led us to the avenue of the fountain. You persuaded us that it would be the safest, fastest route. But it was merely the route you told the Brothers you'd make us take. No wonder they appeared so promptly. They knew exactly where to look!"

Almost all the masks fell away then. William Catto ignored the name Robin called him. He started straight at Magus and there was no mistaking the terrible earnestness of his purpose. At last he lifted a shoulder as if to say, "Why not reveal it? It's of little importance and so are you."

"Yes, I told them. If you hadn't hit on the strategy of using the projectors—if the Brothers had simply attacked and overwhelmed you—they would have let me live."

"You're sure of that," Magus sneered.

"As nearly as a man can be when he's bargained for what counts most. I was willing to take my chances. The Brothers feared you, not me. I warned you long ago, wizard. I told you in clear terms what I wanted. The corporation belongs to me. If I helped you escape, why, you said yourself that you intended to go straight back to Pastora and inform the High Governors that there were no demons here. Destroy superstition that way and they'd have shiploads of colonists onto Lightmark.''

Swiftly he raised his short spear. He placed the tip against Magus' neck.

"Could I let that happen, wizard? Naturally not. Not if I'm to protect what's mine, rebuild it, make it live again. I must have several years of complete control with no interference. That's why I said I'd help you escape; I told you that so I could slip away, find the Brothers and help them dispose of you. Don't accuse me of a lack of scruples. You knew from the beginning what I meant to do.''

Magus' anger became too much. His hand flew up, crashed against the spear, knocked it violently aside. The tip raked his throat as it flew. Blood leaked. He hardly felt it. He shook, uttering one filthy word that summed up his contempt and fury.

Oddly, the word didn't anger Catto. He laughed.

"Well," he roared through his laughter, "well, at least there are no more secrets.''

What was Catto? Madman? In part, but had the balance tipped all the way? Magus suspected that upon the answer to the question hung his own life, and Robin's, and Maya's.

Catto seemed to sense his thoughts.

"I'll tell you this much more, wizard. I've nothing personal against you. You're a brave man. On occasion you've proved yourself a clever one. Now and then I find myself liking you. But if you attack me now or anytime later, I will not try to kill you. Neither will I try to kill your strutting young friend. I'll take this spear and put it into your daughter's belly. She'll go first. I'm fast enough to do it. You know I am. Remember. I won't warn you again.''

And every chaotic plan of attack whirling in Magus' head died stillborn in the chilly sunlight there at the foot of the three soaring ramps.

Robin glanced at Magus. Magus blinked once, shook his head, the tiniest movement, to indicate that Robin should hold his peace. There had to be a way out of the calamitous impasse. But weary as he was, Magus failed to see it.

Maya plainly was exhausted. She was standing up by force of will alone. She couldn't move quickly enough if Catto flung the spear. Magus was not even sure she'd even heard what Catto said. He must wait. He couldn't risk any other course.

With his spear Catto pointed at the cube hanging on the chain around Lantzman's neck. ''Now we can bargain.''

Lantzman closed a protective hand over the bit of metal. He forced a smile. ''Your thinking's muddled, Catto. I have the powering trigger, not you.''

In that moment Magus saw the depth of Catto's lust. The man looked at the little cube with a hunger that was almost sexual.

''I recognize that fact, Philosopher. And I do need that trigger to restart the machines. But a trigger in the shape of a cube presupposes a cube-like aperture, doesn't it? Do you know where to find the aperture for the trigger? You can stand here for years twiddling that cube, but if you don't know how to use if—if you don't know where it fits—what good is it? I know.''

''Of course I know where it fits.''

"You're lying," said Catto.

Magus could see it was so. Lantzman's veneer of confidence cracked. The yellow-booted bravo watched the Philosopher, not comprehending all this, only understanding that things were going against his master. Lantzman's answer faltered:

"The central thinking machine must be in this tower—"

"*Must* be, Philosopher? Then you don't know?"

"I'll find it."

"If you search fifty years," Catto agreed. "How many stories is this building? Two hundred? More? How many pieces of equipment must you explore? Hundreds? Thousands? Hundreds of thousands? Even then you may miss it. How familiar are you with the thing you're seeking?" He smiled. "It's true that I need the powering trigger. Inserted properly, it will start the underground information machines. And the other machines whose tapes turn on the production equipment. And the communications devices with which one of us—or both of us, Lantzman—could speak to other planets. We know there are other worlds out there. Peopled worlds. Waiting for a voice to come out of the dark. There have been no voices since the nuclear rains. There won't be voices again until one corporation like this comes to life. Your little cube can do all that, Lantzman. So you have great power. But I know where the powering trigger must go, because in his day the Prime Manager knew. My ancestor, Lantzman. I know that secret, the one secret you need."

Philosopher Lantzman's eyes watered. "What are you proposing?"

"I'm proposing a coalition. Your trigger, my knowledge."

"You could be lying to me," Lantzman countered. "You may not really know how—"

"Naturally," Catto cut in. "But would I really have come all this way to Lightmark if I were lying? If I didn't know how to use it, any powering trigger would be useless to me. Frankly, I didn't expect you here. I expected to find a powering trigger, though. You tell me they're lost except for yours. Well, even if they aren't, even if you're lying, Lantzman, cooperation is my wisest course. Just as it's yours."

The wind keened low. Magus decided that Catto wasn't bluffing. The tall man was too confident, too quiet now as he prodded.

"Philosopher? Do we have a bargain?"

Lantzman breathed deep. "Equal shares?"

"Of course. We own equal parts of the secret, don't we?"

Magus watched the scene closely. Of the two men, Catto was by far the more controlled. He seemed almost phlegmatic as he waited, letting Lantzman's own greed eat away at hesitation. Lantzman was the weaker. He wanted to believe in Catto. It shone in the moistness of his eyes. With a dry little sigh Lantzman touched the cube on the chain.

"Very well. But can we go immediately?"

"Immediately," Catto replied. "I set only one condition. There are two of you, armed. I don't care for those odds. Send your man"—a hand jerked at the bravo—"to wait for you at the edge of the city. That will be proof of your good faith. One to one. Equals."

Again the Philosopher hesitated. Magus Blacklaw smelled a fearful smell of blood. There was secrecy here somehow. Treachery. Lantzman stroked the little cube, his eyes watering as he gazed out across silver towers and domes.

To his bravo he said, "Wait for me outside the city."

The bravo protested.

"You're in my pay. You'll do as I tell you! Now take yourself away."

The bravo slouched. With a sullen glance at the rest of them he shoved his dagger back into its sheath and started off through the park. His yellow boots became dwindling flashes of color down the avenue.

Catto shielded his eyes. He watched until the bravo was a distant dot. Magnanimous, he indicated the three ramps leading up to the doors of the spire.

"Now, Lantzman, shall we go in and take what's ours?"

The Philosopher shook with emotion as he turned toward the nearest ramp. A step behind, Catto lifted his spear and shoved it into Lantzman's spine.

Lantzman shrieked. Catto shoved the spear in hard. Lantzman fell on his face at the foot of the ramp.

Robin broke into a run. Catto jammed his right boot on Lantzman's back, heaved on the spear. It came out, bloody-bright. Robin lunged for him, Catto was too fast. In two quick jumps he was up the ramp, the spear back over his shoulder ready to cast.

"I'll kill the girl, Dragonard. Stay where you are."

Magus spun toward Maya. She stood alone, unprotected. He started for her.

"Don't, wizard."

Catto's throwing arm was steady. Maya was too far

away. Magus dug his nails into the flesh of his palms and held his ground.

Philosopher Lantzman lifted his head. His brown eyes were dull and full of pain as he stared up the ramp at his murderer. Blood blackened his cloak where the spear had entered. The lower part of his body, hips to ankles, looked oddly boneless.

He let out one fierce, disappointed sob. His forehead struck the ramp. Tears flowed out of his eyes while he died.

"You," Catto said to Robin. "Back away from him."

Robin's gold eyes burned hate. He refused to move. Magus said: "Obey him, Robin. I don't want Maya dead too."

Reluctantly Robin moved off. Catto sidled down the ramp. He bent quickly, twisted with his free hand. He stood up. Wrapped around his hand was the Philosopher's chain with the little metal cube swinging from it.

Catto walked past the body. He thrust the powering trigger into a pocket in his tunic. He gestured Robin backward with the spear.

Robin took another step away. Magus didn't know what Catto planned until it was accomplished. A quick run and the red-haired man was alongside Maya. Her eyes flickered as though she tried to understand what was happening. With Catto's weight against her, she collapsed.

Catto caught her and hoisted her. She hung down over his shoulder, half awake, muttering.

"I hadn't planned on lugging her this way," Catto said, "just close by. I suppose this is safest after all."

He touched the head of his spear to Maya's dangling arm, drawing blood. Then he turned squarely to Magus.

"Don't you want to see Easkod born again, wizard? Come along, come along!

Almost merry, he marched to the nearest ramp and started upward. In Magus' belly sick defeat congealed. His own tiredness, his slow reactions had undone him.

Catto walked fast, up and around the circling ramp. He hailed them from the top near the silver doors.

"Hurry up, wizard. We're going to birth a fantastic offspring. Surely that's of some interest to you."

"He's a madman," Robin whispered.

"It may be," Magus answered. If so, they were done, defeated.

Magus shuffled toward the shining ramp.

XXV

At the head of the ramp William Catto kicked at the silver doors. They opened and he laughed deep in his chest and disappeared inside.

Magus and Robin followed, stepping into a rotunda whose walls and whose ceiling stories above glowed with soft gray radiance. Beneath Magus' boots ran a rich harshness: smooth, sheened white stone interlaced with yellow streakings. A thin coat of dust covered it but couldn't dull its luster.

Marble? Magus had seen the marvelous stuff once or twice on Pastora. It was used to decorate governmental buildings. Tales were told that the wondrously-colored material had come in limited quantities from the First Home unremembered ages ago. This single detail of the stark rotunda filled Magus with unbidden awe. Truly, here was incredible wealth.

In the rotunda's center marble had been used to shape a statue of a slight, mild-faced man in clothing of a queer, ancient cut. The man, obviously of Terran origin, wore peculiar metal-framed lenses in front of his eyes. The lenses were hitched over his ears by extensions of the lens frames.

The statue was a story tall. It was suspended somehow in the rotunda's exact center. Bathed in gray light, it hung a short distance above the floor.

"Who is he?" Magus asked. His voice echoed off the curving walls.

"I've heard it told that this is a representation of the founder of this commercial house," Catto answered. "A man who lived on the First Home long before the Out-riding. His name is unknown."

The benign, almost saintly face of the old gentleman stared unseeing above them. Robin scratched his chin where yellow-white stubble had sprouted. The place had a charged atmosphere, as of vast forces and vaster riches hidden just out of sight.

On Pastora Magus had seen many splendors: palaces of the High Governors, cathedral offices, summer estates of the quality. But none rivaled this marble hall with its strange old statue. He shivered. He tried to remember what he had learned on Lightmark: there was no magic except the magic of mind which humans had created and forgotten.

Catto carried Maya without difficulty as he circled the hovering statue to the rotunda's far wall. There an open staircase ascended in sharp zigzags to a wide door dimly seen up near the very top of the chamber. Though the dusty air inside the tower was chilly, Catto's cheeks ran with sweat. He indicated the steep risers with his spear.

"At the top of this stair, according to my ancestor, there is a room of some size. That will be the end of the search, I think."

And despite his burden he started up the staircase two steps at a time. His boots raised puffs of dust.

Magus tugged Robin's arm. Together the men hurried toward the stairs. Three stories above, Catto was climbing loudly. Magus' heart worked fast inside his chest.

They clattered up the first flight. They kept close to the glowing wall. The open side of the staircase had no rail.

"When the time's right we've got to try to kill him," Robin whispered. "There's no other way."

"There's got to be another way. I won't risk Maya."

"Why are you so sure he'll kill her? Maybe it's nothing but a bluff."

"The sort of bluff I'm unwilling to test. Don't move against him unless I signal you."

Sullen with fury, Robin said nothing. He ran up the next flight and was soon well ahead. Magus dragged along after him.

The staircase doubled back on itself, and again, and once more. The statue in the rotunda was a miniature now, dizzyingly far below. Magus' head began to ache. His eyes blurred.

He rounded a turn, saw Robin waiting to ascend the final flight. He started up.

He slipped, skidding toward the step's outer edge. His right boot plunged into space.

As he fell, he shifted his weight just enough. He slammed face-first athwart two risers. He grabbed hold with slippery fingers. His right leg dangled over the emptiness, the long drop to the yellow-veined marble. . . .

Robin clattered down toward him, caught his arm. Magus struggled to his feet. He lurched over to lean against the wall. Everything swayed, tilted.

At last his eyes shifted into focus. He thrust Robin aside and climbed the last few steps unaided. He was stingingly aware of how slow his reactions had become; how useless he might be in a fight, drained of energy and stamina as he was.

An arch loomed at the top of the stairs. Magus stumbled through. He halted a few steps past the entrance, blinking. Even Robin caught his breath.

Immense and circular, the chamber swept away from them. Its floor was of marble like the rotunda. Its ceiling was two or three stories above. The ceiling glowed softly with the ubiquitous gray light.

Only the arch and one long, plain section interrupted the wall. Everywhere else, hundreds of huge translucent rectangles were massed in groups. The rectangles were separated by banks of meters, faceted lights, calibrated scales housed behind glass. All were dark.

Graceful marble pedestal-chairs were ranged around the floor at various points in front of the banks of equipment. Slightly to the left of the arch, three such chairs rose from a low dais. They faced with cup-shaped seats the stretch of plain wall. This plain wall had a small opening in its center. Around the opening were inlaid panels of some plastic material, etched with the same kind of mysterious yellow ideographs Magus had found on the equipment in Huygens' trunk.

Catto reached the dais. "It wouldn't have been so hard for Philosopher Lantzman to locate the operations center. Of course he didn't know that, did he?"

Grinning, Catto slung Maya into one of the pedestal-chairs. Magus started forward. Catto snapped his head back and forth.

"I think not, wizard. You and your bloodthirsty

226

young friends may stand where you are. Remember, I'm still closest to her.'' And he wigwagged the short spear beneath Maya's chin.

Seething, Magus watched. Catto reached into his tunic and pulled out the powering trigger. Catto ran his thumb across one surface. Then he walked to the aperture in the plain wall. He slipped the cube into it.

Clap! Tiny transparent doors shut over the trigger. Eyes partially closed, Catto stood like a man supplicating his gods.

A minute stretched into two.

Became three.

Four.

Catto's breathing rattled in the quietness. All at once Magus realized the man was mumbling to himself.

"Live. Live. Live. Live."

Magus' spine crawled. The silence was deep, continuing.

"Live. Live. Live. Live."

Nothing happened.

"Live. Live. *Live!*"

Shrieking, Catto wrenched his right arm back to strike the transparent doors.

He went rigid.

His hand opened, a white flower.

Clenched.

His head went back. Laughter poured out. Tears ran down his cheeks.

He began to caper, to dance like a common tavern drunk, whooping.

Stealing up into the worn soles of his jackboots, Magus felt the vibrations.

Robin turned white. A low, far away hum was rising.

With a dazzle, an entire board of faceted lights turned on.

The lights flashed yellow, then green. Catto's face changed colors with them.

Dials pulsed bright blue.

Calibrated scales suffused with red. Indicators shot across their faces.

Magus' legs shook.

"Live!" Catto screamed. "Live, live, live, you beautiful bitch, *live!*"

All the translucent rectangles shone with light.

Now with images.

The images were so dimensionally solid-looking, so exactly colored that Magus could have sworn he was looking at the actual silver structures which the screens showed.

To his right, a motorized grinding. The large section of plain wall began to slide aside. Beyond it, seen through glass, spread the panorama of Easkod City.

Alive.

A dome folded back its roof. Immense gridded paddles shot into the open and turned their faces toward the blaze of sun.

A cylindrical tower telescoped a ten-story antenna straight up.

One outer wall of a ten block square structure dropped into the ground.

Small wheeled carts, driverless, shot into the avenue. Six in a rank, they rolled along ten ranks deep.

Between buildings, the loops and spirals of the multiple pipes opened ports in their surfaces. Through these ports Magus saw black and yellow and white liquids foaming, rushing.

From hundreds of smaller domes more wheeled carts shot out. Some were rod-shaped. Some were teardrop-shaped. The avenues began to fill.

And on the screens, the images changed constantly.

A labyrinth of transparent piping with chemicals smoking inside.

Conveyors rolling, hurling thousands of sealed drums along.

A bank of mixing tanks with silver agitators plunging down through their tops, blades whirling as they disappeared to stir and stir—whatever must be stirred in a dead city suddenly reborn.

Through speakers near the screens came a clatter and a hum of machinery, steadily louder. Another section of gauge-covered wall slid away.

A complex machine with striking keys the size of Magus' fists hammered markings on an endless sheet of thin plastic. The machine spewed the continuous sheet into a large bin below. Catto snatched the end of the sheet, whirled around and around, draping the printed sheet over his shoulder like a cloak.

"She's alive, wizard. Alive and telling us her secrets again." He whacked the sheet with his hand. The striking keys chattered, hammering down, hammering down. The disgorging sheet grew longer, longer, covered with symbols, which characters Magus did not understand.

The screens flashed with dimensional images: one, two, four, six to a screen.

Ten screens: great production lines like the interconnected strands of a spider web.

Thirty screens: vast underground storehouses where the robot vehicles picked off pods of raw materials with extendable silver nippers, stacked them on platforms that hovered but a hand's width off the ground. Loaded, the platforms shot toward ramps and disappeared.

Fifty screens: the skyline of the city, with no building as it had looked when Magus first saw it, but now all sprouting a foresting of paddles, antennae, beacons that revolved, flashing yellow beams that were brilliant even in the burning daylight.

"What do you say now, wizard?" Catto shouted. He tore the plastic sheet, slung a section at Magus. "The knowledge that died in the nuclear rains—there it is. Magic, eh, wizard?"

"Aye," Magus breathed. "There is no magic next to this."

"Do you know something else? I can stay here a year, a century, and the city will care for me. Tend me when I'm ill. Manufacture my food. Entertain me!"

He ran from screen to screen, pointing.

Screen: a rack filled with thousands of glass ampules.

Screen: huge shallow metal trays where porous things the size of cabbages bobbed and bubbled in viscous fluid.

Screen: a picture of souls that suddenly reversed its lights and darks to become the face of three lovely women.

Screen: the multicolored image of a mountebank with painted eyes and nose and cheeks. The camera zoomed back to reveal the mountebank as a painting framed on the wall of a gallery. The lens panned to a framed icescape, a frozen blue sunset on a world totally alien.

Everything a man needed was here in Easkod City.

And the lapping, dissolving screens, the humming, chortling gauges, the flashing winking lights watched it all; regulated it all; showed it all to the man who leaped to the dais and kicked out his legs as he sprawled in a pedestal-chair next to Maya.

William Catto beat his fists on the chair arms in joy.

"Now tell me it wasn't worth a lifetime of eating dung and dying a little every day. It was! It was!"

Out of the chair again, unable to contain his energy. Crossing toward them. Halting only a short distance away.

"Do you know what else the Prime Manager passed down to me, wizard? Knowledge that there are other houses like Easkod, great houses, on planets so far from here that none of the petty minds on Pastora can even conceive of the distance. They'll be waiting, those houses. Waiting for a voice to call them. There are machines in Easkod City to make the calls, wizard. Call across a trillion leagues of stars. One house calling another house. Pooling power. Dragging a whole galaxy up out of the dark. Ruling it, wizard. Oh yes, make no mistake. The men who control the houses that are born again—those men will rule. *Mark me!*" Catto cried as the spittle flew from his lips and his finger stabbed the air. "Those men will *rule!*"

At Magus' side Robin whispered, "Kill him now. While we can."

Dizzy, struggling to stand, Magus waved Robin's words aside. The time had come for his own kind of attack. Never again would William Catto be so struck with happiness as he was at this moment, reveling in the click and chatter and flash and blink of his living, sounding city.

The screens changed, changed, changed. Magus kept his eyes away. The wonders were too astonishing, too drugging. He kept his eyes away from the transparent wall that overlooked the city's unfolding reality. He forced his eyes to Catto's face, and his mind to one fact.

If Catto was not a madman, he trod the line. No common man, no man quite sane, could have dreamed Catto's dream and brought it to reality. Magus was taking the ultimate chance.

He said, "One question. What becomes of us?"

Instantly Catto's face lost its shining joy. The planes flattened. The cheeks grew taut above his red moustaches. The eyes turned calculatingly sane.

Or was the sanity a veneer? No matter. The danger was identical.

"You cannot leave," Catto said. "I've told you that before."

"Prisoners, all our days? Is that what it's to be?"

"Don't be so bitter. There's a lot for you here. The machines will help retard my own aging, but I still won't live forever. Neither will I be able to use all the wealth I'll create from this place after I call the other great houses and find those that are alive and we start to rebuild trade." A sidewise glance at the girl slumped on the pedestal-chair. "I want sons and daughters. Your girl could bear them just as well—no, wait. Hear me out. My manner of offering may be crude. I'm tired. Tired as you are. But think. There's more than enough here. I'll share it with you. Yes, and with your daughter. Even with that not-too-bright young man glowering behind you. Think the offer over well before you reject it. You know how far I've come. You know how far I mean to go before I die. Think carefully about what you could have." He slashed the spear at the blinding gauges, the shining screens, the city.

The terrible hell of it was, Magus believed him.

Power.

Security.

So accessible, so simple to seize—

But it wasn't entirely unpleasant. In his mind's eye he saw himself accepting Catto's offer. Reaching the end of a torturous road he and Maya had traveled too long.

Catto was grinning. Magus opened his lips to speak. Something stopped him. One or two simple memories: a Brother killed without provocation; Philosopher Lantzman bleeding through his back, astonished, betrayed, murdered.

"Join forces? No thank you."

"I'm a murderer, is that what you're thinking?"

"I only know part of you, Catto. That part's the murderer. As for the rest—"

The words remained unspoken. *The rest* would determine whether or not they lived or died.

"Any dream worth seizing, wizard, is worth seizing regardless of the price."

"On that we differ."

Catto tightened his hand around the shaft of the spear. "You leave me no choice but to kill you."

"There's one other choice. You owe me something."

Up came Catto's head, arrogant, the moustaches like fire.

"I owe you *nothing*."

"Yes, you do. You owe your life. You'd have died

at the fountain if it hadn't been for me.''All at once Catto's eyes dulled.

His shoulders sloped. His skin looked wan as the light of the walls. For the first time Magus noticed gray hairs, just a few, shot through the man's red hair.

The beast was struggling. Catto held his spear tightly. All the color drained from his hand. In his eyes the beast crawled free.

Looked out.

Hated.

Then slowly slunk away.

"Goddamn you," Catto said. "You'll tell them on Pastora, won't you? Tell them about this place—"

"Yes. And they'll come."

"All right—all right, let them! There are still Brothers out on the plain. Frightened of the city's magic. I'll let them guard me. Guard the city. I can frighten them into it—yes! Tell them about me on Pastora! Tell them there are no demons! Let them load the ships with fools and send them here. Some will refuse to join me. But of a sudden it strikes me that I may not have much of a fight on my hands after all.''

Catto walked to Magus. A pace behind, Robin shifted warily, gold eyes watching. Catto leaned close to Magus. His breath was rotten.

"I don't thing the burghers of Pastora will struggle overmuch against me when they get here. I'll control this place. I can promise them what I promised you. Wealth. Wealth through trade. They'll not be so clever and discerning as you. They'll not refuse me. I can make them gods again, with only one stipulation. That they obey me. I think they will. I think they'll trade my rewards for their freedom and I'll end up ruling both the worlds under Graphos.''

With a sad voice Magus answered, "I don't doubt you're right."

"It makes no difference to you?"

"I'll be long dead. I have no great desire to change history."

"You scrupulous fool, you already have."

With a peculiar dignity, Magus dusted his hands on the silver-stitched sash around his waist. It was torn in several places. Well, no matter. It would never need to be mended again.

A little line of sweat trickled down from his left ear. "I'll take my daughter now."

"What about the scientific apparatus? Do you still want those too?"

"Would it matter?"

"No. You stretch my generosity thin already. Your miserable lives are gift enough."

"Yes," said Magus, meaning every word. "They are."

"Ignorant bastard. But I suppose you can't expect any more from a charlatan." Turning abruptly, he walked back to the glowing screens.

Carefully Magus slipped to the dais. He lifted Maya. Her weight was almost unbearable.

He managed to hoist her onto his shoulder. He and Robin walked out through the arch. Against the chatter and hum, Catto was talking to himself.

They crept down the staircase. They crossed the rotunda. They went swiftly down the graceful ramp and along the avenues, keeping to the side to avoid being run over by the trains of little pilotless vehicles. Easkod City bustled, but inhumanly.

Magus plodded. Several times he refused Robin's offer of help. He wanted his daughter's weight against his shoulder. The pilotless vehicles bumped by, sounding loud horns. Within silver buildings machines clacked, working at unguessable labors.

"I thought for certain he'd kill us," Robin said at length.

"I thought so too. I had to gamble against it. There was no other way."

"The man's filth. Power-hungry filth."

"Don't be so quick to judge, Robin. Not until you've lived as long as he has, the way he has, wanting what he wants. He was a man when he could have been an animal. He let us go. Give him that."

Grumbling, Robin went silent. They walked on up the avenue past the last of the silver buildings. Magus was tired. Sick of thinking. Sick of fighting. He wanted only to reach the skysled and close his eyes.

The plain stretched ahead. It glared in the sun. He began to hum a tavern air and they passed out of Easkod City without looking back.

XXVI

LONG BEFORE they reached the skysled Magus' head throbbed with fever. But he refused to stop.

All day, they plodded up the V-shaped plain. He let Robin carry Maya now, though the removal of the burden didn't help much.

He saw multiple images in the thickening twilight. He smelled his own unwashed stink, felt the crawling itch of dirt in his beard, his ears, his very pores. His empty belly snapped and gurgled at him. Robin looked no better. Dust had turned his yellow-white hair the color of ashes. His cheeks trickled with sweat.

The moon of Lightmark sailed up. The evening grew cool. They kept marching.

About an hour after dark, Magus saw shapes on one of the ridges. Ahead, slogging ahead with Maya over his shoulder, Robin failed to see that they were being watched.

Magus struggled to catch up. He pointed at the ridgeline.

Horny-headed in silhouette against the sparkling stars, Brothers watched in groups of three or four. On the far side of the ridge Magus thought he heard beasts stamping.

"Make no sign you see them," Magus said. "Walk straight on. Let's hope they're frightened of us since we took their leader away."

The men kept moving. The Brothers never stirred. They simply watched, as though they wanted to see gods passing by.

After a while Magus started humming again. He could barely keep a tune. He knew his legs wouldn't hold out another ten steps. Somehow they did. Robin peered back over his shoulder.

"They're gone. The ridges are empty."

Magus uttered a croaking laugh. From far away the wind carried the drumming of many beasts. This dwindled. Like specters the two ragged, filthy men staggered on.

Sunrise. The blazing corona of Graphos on the horizon brought a yell from Robin. The gray-blue skysled rested where they had left it. The sun fell against its nearer side and cast a long shadow on the other. Magus tramped ahead, swaying, snorting, almost out of his senses.

Robin was still carrying Maya. He was a few paces behind. Magus stumbled to the craft. He leaned his head against the metal skin a moment. Then he turned to his right, into the sun. Blinded, he groped for the hatch and began to undo it.

Out of the sun a spindly figure slipped, fragmented, diffuse as something seen through a prism. Magus swiped his forearm over his eyes.

What *was* the odd shape sliding toward him? Arms, legs, a head. But blurred out of proportion.

He knew it was his fever altering reality, fought himself awake.

Lantzman's last bravo crept along the side of the skysled.

Magus understood. The man had been hiding in the shadows on the craft's far side. The bravo slid his right hand along the metal skin. In his left his dagger flashed. His eyes were huge, stupid, hungry above his sprouted beard. He dragged his yellow-booted feet in the shale, lips peeled back like a ravening animal.

"Been waiting. Figured you were the only ones left when the Philosopher didn't come back."

"The Philosopher is dead," Magus said. "We'll carry you to Pastora if you want."

"You'd only hand me to the Governors. I'll just go myself, once you show me how to run this piece of tin. Never should of hired on to that crazy man. Never should of done it."

The bravo licked his lips. Magus realized the man was sun-struck.

"Come on, come on!" The bravo twisted his dagger in an angry little circle. "Open the hatch and show me how it works or I'll slit you—"

The bravo's eyes bulged, looking somewhere past Magus' shoulder. How had he failed to see Robin before? But he saw him now.

The bravo shouted, spittle flying from between his teeth. He ran straight to Magus to kill him.

Magus stepped back. His head struck the skysled hull. He tried to dodge aside but the bravo was on him, slavering, raving, the dagger cutting down.

Metal ate into the right side of his throat, low near his shoulder muscles. Pain ripped him. He doubled over.

Magus had a kaleidoscope view of the skysled, the bravo's yellow boots, the dagger swinging up again toward the underside of his chin. Graphos fumed and flamed in the sky. Magus' legs buckled. He fell facefirst in the shale.

Somewhere men grunted and spat. He no longer cared. Resting, he let the blood from his neck drain over him. Graphos wormed inside his eyes and went nova, bringing total dark.

A stinging scent in his nostrils. A cool slickness when he reached to touch his own bare shoulder. A crosshatch of reinforcing members there above him. With difficulty he focused his eyes.

"Lie easy, Magus."

That voice, To whom did it belong? He should know. He tried to turn his head. A fit of fever seized him, making his teeth rattle.

"Lie easy. In the compartment for the book-rolls there was one that explained the medical kit. I've stopped the blood with some kind of spray—"

A hand appeared in his line of sight. It held a melon-shaped object of tawny plastic with a ring of spray nozzles around the top.

"What—happened?"

"I took his knife away and killed him. He nearly killed you before I got to him."

Gold eyes. Steady, weary. Magus recognized the cross members above Robin. He knew he was safely inside the skysled.

He tried to utter thanks. No use. He knew it was over.

He closed his eyes and slept.

But of course it wasn't over. The task of lifting the skysled from Lightmark remained.

Magus left this chiefly to Robin, offering a comment now and then from his place in the center launch chair. The padding felt good against his back.

His belly was filled. They'd broken out fresh stores of the gummy nutrient after he woke up an hour ago. Lightmark's dusk brushed at the ports, muting the colors of the harsh landscape.

Robin set the controls by following the book-roll on the subject. At length he threw the last lever and settled into the launch chair to Magus' left.

In the right-hand chair Maya breathed deeply. She was sleeping again. She'd wakened once a few minutes ago. She'd spoken to Magus, recognizing him before weariness caught her again. She looked strangely beautiful despite the accumulation of dirt on her face and the frightful tangle of her russet hair.

Magus turned away, overcome with a piercing melancholy.

He'd meant to be rich when he came home from Lightmark. Rich so that Maya would never fret or fear or lack security again. And he was returning to Pastora less than a whole man himself. His wound throbbed. It smelled faintly unclean despite the medicinal dressing Robin had sprayed on it.

The skysled's prow lurched upward sharply. A ratcheting sound penetrated the control canopy. There was a second lurch.

"That should be the built-in cradle extending itself," Robin said.

"The procedure's all in the book-roll?"

"Fortunately."

Up went the prow again. The skysled pointed at the sky.

The little colored lights on the curved console

winked faster. The illuminated dial in the center swept off intervals of time with its long red hand. The skysled began to rattle and vibrate. Magus heard the whirring of the think-machines as they set the path home.

The red hand chopped off the last interval. Noise burst against his eardrums. Force wrenched against his face, peeling his lips from his teeth, folding his cheeks into unnatural pockets. The skysled roared toward the stars.

The craft slid into its launching orbit, racing from darkness around into the glare of the day side.

"Sir?"

Magus barely heard. He was watching the shimmer of sun against the transparent port.

"Sir?"

Magus turned his head. Robin was watching him with a strange intensity. Magus wondered why the lad was worrying.

True, the skysled was emitting various creaks and groans suggestive of fatigued materials. But Magus had reached the point where perils were regarded as cool curiosities. He'd burned out his own capacity for terror.

Then it struck that Robin Dragonard had never called him *sir* before.

"What do you want?" he asked.

"I—there's no proper time for this. But if we reach Pastora . . ."

"I don't intend to discuss our future. It died on Lightmark when we left all the apparatus behind."

"Maya could have one, sire. I mean to marry her."

It startled Magus out of his depression. He turned his head against the chair's thick padding. Robin still watched him. *The lad's scared! Kills a bravo one moment, trembles the next.*

But then of course this is the traditional ritual, isn't it? Querying the father. Odd place for it, Magus thought as the skysled flashed from the day side into the murk of night, picking up velocity on this final orbital pass.

Robin took his silence to mean a negative reaction. He fisted his right hand, held it up before Magus' face.

Magus stared at the gold ring on Robin's little finger. Ah yes, the old symbol. Etched into the oval black stone. Mythic animals. Snarling lion, rising phoenix. The name Dragonard had been written in many a book-roll.

"I come from a good house," Robin said. "There were great men in the house before me. It'll be so again."

"I'm not denying—"

"I may not be the brightest of them, or the cleverest, but . . ."

"There's nothing wrong with you, Robin. For one thing you've got courage in plenty. For a man who grew up on Pastora—well, that means something."

But wasn't he like Robin? All he had was a sharp mind and a ready sword and what had it netted him? Exactly nothing save their lives and a return to Pastora. They seemed small rewards.

"Are you feeling all right?" Robin asked.

"Damn you, of course I'm feeling—"

And suddenly Magus was sitting up, startled, wrathful, astonished at how clearheaded he did feel. The depression sloughed away.

"My question, sir—"

"Marry her if she'll have you." Magus sniffed. "I suppose she will."

Laughing, Robin leaned back in his launch chair. Magus leaned back in similar fashion. Amazing, how refreshed he felt. All at once. He sighed.

Perhaps he'd chased an illusion. Perhaps of all the discoveries he'd made on Lightmark the most important was this: he'd never have a comfortable life. He was probably fated to be a wandering mounteback all his days. Was that so bad?

At least now Maya would be protected. Perhaps he'd have grandchildren he could dandle, telling tales of how he exorcised an entire planet with silks and a sword and balls of green fire. And his wits. Ah, yes, his wits. A man could be proud of that, couldn't he?

Of course his grandchildren would bear a different name. Dragonard. A good name. An old name. A name with the ring of history to it. Who knew? From Maya and Robin might spring another Dragonard, or a whole new clan of them, to make history again.

William Catto said that this galaxy with its far-hung lights, its glowing worlds, would come to life. There could be places for the Dragonards to write their names large.

And of course he'd completely forgotten Serafina.

Serafina. Charming thought. Full-bosomed. Companionable. A widow of warmth and merry eagerness. A shame that she must languish in New Delft, unloved and unwarmed on winter nights when the bells rang lonely across the moors of Pastora. He'd fix that. He'd visit her as soon as—

Patterns of lights, yellow, green, blue, white, vermilion, lapped across the inner surface of the control canopy above them. The lights shone, blinked, trembled and just as quickly as they had come, they vanished.

"Easkod City," Robin said. "Those must be the lights, shining up from below."

"But we must be leagues above the city. How could there be lights powerful enough to—"

There could be such lights among the wonders. He knew that now.

The skysled changed direction, aiming out toward the stars.

"I still say Catto's a madman," Robin grumbled. "He won't be able to rebuild a hundred worlds, let alone one."

"Perhaps the task takes a madman. Did you stop to think of that?"

Magus felt drowsy. He touched his daughter's cheek. Then he laced his hands over his belly. His eyelids grew heavy. The skysled shot among the stars, homeward bound.

Magus murmured, "Who knows what Catto can do? I'll ask my grandchildren in a couple of hundred years."

Then the wizard fell asleep.

XXVII

THUS came to power William Catto, ancestor of the first
Lord of the exchange to bear the hereditary title Easkod
I in the later days when the Lords ruled their reborn
houses in mighty confederation.

Thus out of dark did a part of II Galaxy rise toward
truth's light.

Thus did Magus Blacklaw pass into legend on Pastora, and mingle his blood into the red stream of the
House of Dragonard.

WINNER OF
THE HUGO AWARD
AND THE
NEBULA AWARD
FOR BEST
SCIENCE FICTION
NOVEL OF
THE YEAR

*04594 **Babel 17** Delany $1.50	
*05476 **Best Science Fiction of the Year** Del Rey $1.25	
06218 **The Big Time** Leiber $1.25	
*10623 **City** Simak $1.75	
16649 **The Dragon Masters** Vance $1.50	
16704 **Dream Master** Zelazny $1.50	
19683 **The Einstein Intersection** Delany $1.50	
24903 **Four For Tomorrow** Zelazny $1.50	
47071 **The Last Castle** Vance 95¢	
47803 **Left Hand of Darkness** Leguin $1.95	
72784 **Rite of Passage** Panshin $1.50	
79173 **Swords and Deviltry** Leiber $1.50	
80694 **This Immortal** Zelazny $1.50	

Available wherever paperbacks are sold or use this coupon.

ace books, (Dept. MM) Box 576, Times Square Station
New York, N.Y. 10036
Please send me titles checked above.

I enclose $ . . . . Add 35c handling fee per copy.

Name . . . .

Address . . . .

City . . . . State . . . . Zip . . . .